JAMES PATTERSON
BOOKSHOTS

Dear Reader,

You're about to experience a revolution in reading—BookShots.

BookShots are a whole new kind of book—100 percent story-driven, no fluff, always under $5.

I've written or co-written nearly all the BookShots and they're among my best novels of any length.

At 150 pages or fewer, BookShots can be read in a night, on a commute, or even on your cell phone during breaks at work.

I hope you enjoy *The Medical Examiner*.

All my best,

James Patterson

P.S.

For special offers an   please go to

D0035780

BOOK**SHOTS**

BOOK**SHOTS**
Flames

THE MEDICAL EXAMINER

A WOMEN'S MURDER CLUB STORY

JAMES PATTERSON
WITH MAXINE PAETRO

BOOK**SHOTS**

Little, Brown and Company

New York Boston London

Copyright © 2017 by James Patterson

Hachette Book Group supports the right to free expression and the value of copyright. The purpose of copyright is to encourage writers and artists to produce the creative works that enrich our culture.

The scanning, uploading, and distribution of this book without permission is a theft of the author's intellectual property. If you would like permission to use material from the book (other than for review purposes), please contact permissions@hbgusa.com. Thank you for your support of the author's rights.

BookShots / Little, Brown and Company
Hachette Book Group
1290 Avenue of the Americas, New York, NY 10104
bookshots.com

First Edition: August 2017

BookShots is an imprint of Little, Brown and Company, a division of Hachette Book Group, Inc. The Little, Brown name and logo are trademarks of Hachette Book Group, Inc. The BookShots name and logo are trademarks of JBP Business, LLC.

The publisher is not responsible for websites (or their content) that are not owned by the publisher.

The Hachette Speakers Bureau provides a wide range of authors for speaking events. To find out more, go to hachettespeakersbureau.com or call (866) 376-6591.

ISBN 978-0-316-50482-9
LCCN 2017938656

10 9 8 7 6 5 4 3 2 1

LSC-C

Printed in the United States of America

THE MEDICAL EXAMINER

PROLOGUE

INSPECTOR RICHARD CONKLIN WAS conducting what should have been a straightforward interview with a female victim. The woman was the only known witness to a homicide.

But Mrs. Joan Murphy, the subject, was not making Conklin's job any easier. She was understandably distraught, traumatized, and possibly a bit squirrelly. As a result, she'd taken the interview straight off road, through the deep woods, and directly over a cliff.

She'd seen nothing. She couldn't remember anything. And she didn't understand why she was being interviewed by a cop in the first place.

"Why am I even here?"

The question made Conklin immediately wonder: *What is she hiding?*

They were in a hospital room at St. Francis Memorial. Mrs. Murphy was reclining in a bed with a sling around her right arm. She was in her mid-forties and was highly agitated. Her face was so tightly drawn that Conklin thought she might have had too much cosmetic surgery. Either that, or this was what the aftereffects of a near-death experience looked like.

Currently, Mrs. Murphy was shooting looks around the hospital room as if she were about to bolt through the window. It reminded Conklin of that viral video of the deer who'd wandered into a convenience store, then leapt over the cash register and the pretzel rack before finally crashing through the plate-glass windows.

"Mrs. Murphy," he said.

"Call me Joan."

A nurse came through the door, saying, "How are we feeling, Mrs. Murphy? Open up for me, please." She stuck a thermometer under Mrs. Murphy's tongue, and after a minute, she read the numbers and made a note on the chart.

"Everything's normal," she said, brightly.

Conklin thought, *Easy for you to say.*

He turned back to the woman in the bed and said, "Joan, it kills me to see you so upset. I fully comprehend that getting shot, especially under your conditions, would shake anyone up. That's why I hope you understand that I have to find out what happened to you."

Mrs. Murphy was not a suspect. She was not under arrest. Conklin had assured her that if she asked him to leave the room, he would do it. No problem.

But that wasn't what he wanted. He wanted to understand the circumstances that had victimized this woman and had killed the man who had been found with her.

He had to figure out what kind of case it was so he could nab the culprit.

"Don't worry. I'm not afraid of you, Richard," Joan told him, looking past him and out the window. "It's everything you've told me that's upsetting me. I don't remember having a dead body beside me. I don't remember much of anything, but I do think I would remember that. Honestly, I don't think it even happened."

She shook her head desperately and the tears flew off her cheeks. She dropped her chin to her chest and her shoulders heaved with sobs.

Conklin reached for a box of tissues and offered them to his disconsolate subject, who was melting down in front of him.

He inched his chair closer to the bed and said, "Joan, please try to understand. It did happen. We have the body. Do you want to see him?"

She plucked a tissue from the box, patted her eyes, and blew her nose.

"Must I?"

Conklin said, "I think it would be best. It might jog your memory. Look, I'll stay with you and you can lean on me."

"And then you'll drive me straight home?"

"I sure will. I'll even put the sirens on."

FORTY-EIGHT HOURS EARLIER

CHAPTER 1

CINDY THOMAS, SENIOR CRIME reporter at the *San Francisco Chronicle,* breezed through the front door of Susie's Café. She threaded her way through the raucous crowd in the front room, past the steel drum band and the crowded bar, and headed down the corridor to the back room. It was packed to the walls with the Saturday-night dinner set.

She saw an empty booth and a recently vacated table, and asked a busboy for help as she shoved the table up against the booth.

"How many people are coming?" he asked her.

"Six," she told him. "I hope the kitchen doesn't run out of the mango chicken. That's our favorite."

Four of the six were herself and her closest friends in the Women's Murder Club. The other members were Lindsay Boxer, Homicide, SFPD; Claire Washburn, chief medical examiner; and Yuki Castellano, assistant DA. Tonight, the two additional seats would be for Lindsay's husband, Joe Molinari, and Cindy's own beloved fiancé, Rich Conklin. Rich was also Lindsay's partner on the job.

It had been a joke when Cindy dubbed the four of them the

Women's Murder Club years ago, but the name had stuck because they liked it. The girls regularly gathered at Susie's, their clubhouse, in order to vent, brainstorm, and fill up on spicy Caribbean food and draft beer. It was nice to go with the "don't worry, be happy" flow every once in a while.

Laughs were definitely on the menu tonight.

Lindsay had been pulling double shifts at her high-stress job, and recently had been put on a harrowing assignment with the antiterrorism task force. Her husband, Joe Molinari, was still recovering from injuries he'd received in a terrorist bombing related to that very case.

That was probably why Lindsay's sister offered to take their little girl, Julie, home with her and her own little girls for the week. Everything was all set. Lindsay and Joe were leaving in the morning for a well-earned vacation in Mendocino, a small-town escape 150 miles north of San Francisco.

Cindy was excited for them. She ordered beer and chips for the table and had settled into the banquette when Lindsay and Joe arrived. They all hugged, and then the tall blond cop and her hunky husband slid into the booth.

Lindsay said, "I think I'm going to fall asleep in the car and then stay in bed for the entire week. It's inevitable."

Joe put an arm around Lindsay, pulled her close, and said, "If that's the case, there will be no complaints from me."

"All righhhht," said Cindy. Beer was poured into frosted mugs, and Cindy made the first toast. "To rain," she said. "Gentle, pattering rain and no Wi-Fi reception."

"Let's drink to that," said Lindsay.

Glass clinked, Lindsay gulped some beer, and after setting down her mug, she asked Cindy, "You sure you're up to taking care of Martha? She's used to being the boss, you know."

Lindsay was referring to her family's best dog friend, an aging border collie who had pulled a tendon and was under doctor's orders for bed rest.

"I think I can handle it. After all, I, too, am used to being the boss," Cindy said with a wink.

"You? Bossy? You must be joking," said Lindsay.

Cindy was known to be more pit bull than pussycat. She and Lindsay were still snickering about it when Claire Washburn arrived.

Claire emphatically endorsed Lindsay's upcoming week of R & R. She slid into the booth next to her, saying, "I know I'm going to miss you to death, but I'm not going to call you. And I mean, no way, no how, not for any reason. Seriously. This week, nothing but radio silence, okay?"

Before Lindsay could answer, Rich Conklin arrived tableside, stepping on Claire's laugh line. He said hey to his friends and bent down to give Cindy a kiss as Yuki danced into the room, singing along with the Caribbean tune. Rich gave her the seat next to Cindy and pulled up a chair for himself.

Yuki ordered her first margarita of the evening, and the dinner orders went in after that. Even though the upbeat music was plinking loudly and laughter and applause made conversation challenging, Cindy felt a tremendous pleasure in this gathering of close friends. The gang was all here and the evening felt like a group hug. It was the kind of night out that she wanted to soak up and remember forever.

She wouldn't change a thing.

CHAPTER 2

ON MONDAY MORNING, CLAIRE arrived at the medical examiner's office—her office—at ten before eight.

As she walked through the reception room, she was still transitioning from her home to her work mindset. Her thoughts hopscotched from the pressure of back-to-school week with her youngest kiddo, her grumpy husband, who was looking toward early retirement, and the transmission fluid she needed for her car. Not to mention the strong coffee and donut she needed to help her shift her own gears.

She had just hung her coat behind her door when Dr. Harrison, the on-call ME handling the night shift, knocked on the door frame to her office.

"Morning, Bernard. What's the latest?" she asked her number two.

"First, we had a bad accident on the freeway at around midnight last night," he told her. "A car jumped the median and T-boned a family that was coming home from grandma's house. There were three fatalities. One of the children is in the emergency room."

"Oh, damn."

"Fifteen minutes after we'd admitted the car crash victims, two more fatalities came in. It's all in here," he said, waggling a folder containing a sheaf of notes. "I was able to get through two of the freeway postmortems and left the rest for you."

"So you've left three patients for me, you're saying?"

"You don't get paid the big bucks for the easy jobs."

She smiled at their inside joke. There were no big bucks to be found in civil service, but Claire loved what she did. She wouldn't have it any other way.

Dr. H. kept filling her in. "Bunny's here, and so is Mallory. Greg is running late, and I have a headache the size of a beach ball."

"Go home," she told him. "Take an aspirin and get some sleep."

"Don't have to tell me twice, Doc," he said. "Watch out for my vapor trail."

He handed his notes to Claire. She took them with her to the kitchenette, where she poured coffee, snagged the one chocolate donut in the box, and ate her second breakfast at the small square table. Her two assistants, Bunny Ellis and Mallory Keane, came in and took turns filling her in on the horrible car crash.

Bunny's eyes were welling up as she said, "One's just a little kid, Doctor. He's only eight."

Claire said, "I know, I know, Bunny. We never get used to the kids."

Then Claire gowned up and went into the cool room with

Bunny at her elbow. Mallory trailed close behind them. Claire opened the refrigerator drawer that contained the remains of the young boy. He should have been getting on a school bus next week.

"I'm so sorry, Sean Morrison," Claire said to the dead child. "I know a lot of people are going to miss you terribly."

She turned to Bunny and asked, "Are his parents here?"

"Dr. H. did the posts on his mom and dad. His sister is at Metro in serious condition."

"And the driver?" Claire asked.

"Drunk, and texting while driving. He just walked away. From what I heard, there was hardly a scratch on him."

Bunny wheeled a stretcher over to young Sean's drawer. As she helped Claire lift the child's body, they heard a sound that was part moan, part shriek.

"Bunny? What the hell was that?"

"It wasn't me. Could it have been the wheels squeaking, maybe?"

Claire turned around and asked, "Mallory? Was that you?"

"What? No. I didn't hear nothing, and I didn't say nothing either."

The three women stood very still. When they were sure they heard only the sounds of their own breathing, they resumed moving the little boy's body to the gurney.

But then there was another moan, and this time it was followed by a fit of coughing. Together, Claire and Bunny converged on the second level of shelves, four feet off the floor.

Mallory pointed to the drawer at the far end. Claire pulled on the handle—and jumped back.

The body bag inside the drawer was moving.

Claire screamed, surprising herself, and after that, she stepped up and pulled down the body bag zipper. A bloody arm protruded from the bag. A body stirred within and then spoke.

"What kind of nightmare is this?"

CHAPTER 3

THAT MORNING, CINDY OPENED the front door to Lindsay and Joe's airy three-bedroom apartment on Lake Street.

Martha was lying in the living room next to Joe's big chair, where she had a clear view of the doorway. As soon as she saw Cindy, she got to her feet and, with her tail wagging, trotted over to her. It took a couple of tries for Martha to get up onto her hind legs, so Cindy bent down to hug her and hold her up.

"Hey, Sweet Martha. Howsa good girl? Wanna go for a walk?"

Cindy grabbed a paper bag from the counter, found the collar and leash on a hook by the door, and took Martha for a slow but productive stroll on 12th Street. She knew there wasn't very much traffic there, so it'd be a safe route for the two of them.

While they were walking, Cindy talked to Martha, reciting two headlines for a story she had to turn in in the next hour. She asked her which one she liked better, but Martha was noncommittal. After Martha did her business and Cindy bagged it, the duo returned to Lindsay's apartment.

Cindy was pouring dog chow into Martha's bowl, concentrating so she didn't get kibble all over the floor, when the phone rang. She knew it was going to be Lindsay, checking on her. Ha! She reached for the phone.

"Linds?"

"No, it's Claire. Oh, damn it to hell! Sorry, Cindy. I just speed-dialed Lindsay. I forgot. Force of habit."

Cindy kept the phone to her ear as she filled Martha's water bowl in the sink. When Claire explained why she had called, Cindy almost dropped the phone. She shut off the water to make sure that she'd heard her friend correctly.

"Say that again?"

Then Cindy said, "What? Ha. Good one, Claire."

Claire's voice came over the earpiece—loud. "I'm not making this up. Look, I've got to go."

Cindy said, "I'm on my way. Jesus, Claire. I'm coming."

"No, Cindy."

"Yes, Claire. I'm ten minutes away."

CHAPTER 4

THE WOMAN WHO HAD been logged into the morgue as deceased helped Claire and her assistants get her own body out of the bag. She moved into a sitting position inside the drawer. This, whatever it was, was very, very disturbing. In all her years as a medical examiner, Claire had never seen anything like it. The body in front of her had literally come back from the dead.

Was this a prank? A mistake? A true zombie?

She said, "Bunny, get my kit. Mallory, call an ambulance."

The woman sitting in the drawer was naked, and blood was smeared all over her body. She was holding her left arm at her elbow and was wincing in pain.

Claire said, "My name is Dr. Washburn. May I help you? What hurts? Okay, now. Here we go."

Claire peeled the woman's hand away from her shoulder and saw a gunshot wound that went from the front straight through to the back. It was called a through-and-through. Because the woman was able to move her arm, it looked as though no bones had been broken. Thank goodness.

She asked, "Can you tell me your name?"

"I should wake up now," said the woman in the drawer. "This has to be a dream. This is a nightmare for the ages."

"You're in the medical examiner's office. You're going to be fine," Claire said. "We're going to get you off of that skinny little bed, right now."

Claire was still shocked that the woman in the drawer was alive, but she was starting to get some perspective. This wasn't the first time in history that a convincingly dead person had revived himself or herself inside a morgue—or a coffin. There were cases in the nineteenth century where people overdosed on barbiturates and were presumed dead, even though they had, instead, fallen into a deathlike state. Some of the time, they "came back to life" before burial.

Claire wondered if there was a modern drug affecting the woman in front of her, but then she remembered that there was a condition called catalepsy.

Could the bloody woman have that disorder?

Claire knew that people who suffer from catalepsy go into a dead-not-dead state, with slow breathing and a weak pulse. Their muscles go rigid, and sometimes they lose sensation in their body. Claire recalled from something she had read long ago that catalepsy could be triggered by disease, certain drugs, or traumatic shock. And if the "undead" was cooled down—for instance, by being stored inside a morgue's cold room—the brain would remain functional until death took over or the person awoke.

In today's high-tech medical environment, it would be hard to mistake catalepsy for death. But this woman appeared to be an exception to the rule.

The patient was clearly not dead.

CHAPTER 5

THE WOMAN IN THE drawer stretched out her good arm, and Claire and Bunny helped her to a standing position.

Claire's spot assessment was that this poor thing was middle-aged and bone-thin. She'd been shot and was lucky to be breathing.

Claire also saw that another bullet had grazed her hip. Like the shot to her shoulder, it wasn't life-threatening.

Would this lady's good luck continue? Or would bad luck send her back in the drawer?

Bunny and Mallory helped the woman onto a stretcher and pulled a sheet up to her shoulders while Claire checked her vitals. The woman was breathing without assistance. Her pulse was slow, but her heart was beating regularly. Her wounds weren't bleeding and she had spoken, which is always a good sign.

Claire put her stethoscope away, and the woman's eyelids suddenly flew open. The woman drew back, afraid. It was as though she'd forgotten she'd been awake just moments ago.

"Who are you?" she gasped. "Where am I?"

Claire introduced herself again and ordered someone to get water. Then she asked, "What's your name?"

"My name?"

After a few long seconds, the woman said, "I'm Joan Murphy. Did you say this is a morgue? What am I doing here?"

"I was hoping you could tell me, Miss Murphy."

"Call me Joan. My shoulder. It hurts."

"Actually, medically, that's a good sign. You took a bullet, Joan, so it's natural for your body to be reacting to the pain. Do you know who shot you?"

"What day is it?" Joan asked.

"Monday. It's about eight thirty in the morning."

"So yesterday was Sunday?"

"That's right."

"Well, I woke up in my own house. I had breakfast and watched the news shows with my husband—my husband. Someone has to call Robert."

"Of course. We will. Right away."

Joan Murphy recited numbers and Mallory wrote them down.

Then Claire said to her patient, "Joan, an ambulance is on the way. You need emergency medical attention and I'm not equipped to do that for you here."

"If I could just get dressed," said Joan.

Just then, the swinging doors to the autopsy suite blew wide open.

And here was Cindy, as promised. She was breathing hard

as she hurried over to Claire and the woman lying on the stretcher.

"I'm Cindy Thomas," she said to the patient. "I hope you're feeling better. What an ordeal, right?"

Then Cindy turned to Claire and said, "What did I miss?"

"I don't remember anything," said Joan Murphy. "But obviously, I was murdered. Well, it was attempted murder, I suppose. That's all I know."

CHAPTER 6

THE IRREPRESSIBLE CINDY THOMAS had just breathlessly materialized in Claire Washburn's autopsy suite, and Claire wasn't pleased. Not in the slightest.

Claire said, "Seriously, Cindy? Didn't I say no?"

She was planning to spin her friend around and march her straight out when the doors to the ambulance bay banged open.

Bunny shouted to the EMTs, "Hurry. She's in there."

The EMTs burst into the cold room with a stretcher in tow.

"What have we got, Doctor?" asked an EMT. The name W. Watson was appliquéd on his shirt.

Claire said to Watson, "This is Mrs. Murphy."

"Hello," Joan said. "The rumors of my demise have been wildly exaggerated."

Watson cracked a smile.

"She was brought in just after midnight," Claire continued. "She has a gunshot wound to the shoulder and a bullet graze on her hip. She revived on her own fifteen minutes ago and needs emergency care ASAP."

Watson said, "You're not kidding."

Mallory went to Mrs. Murphy and patted her hand.

"I left a message for your husband," she said. "I told him you were on the way to Saint Francis Memorial Hospital."

"How ya doing, Mrs. Murphy?" EMT Watson asked. "We're going to give you a nice smooth ride. And we'll get there faster than a speeding bullet." Then the EMTs helped the gunshot victim onto their gurney and wheeled her out to the ambulance.

The doors closed behind them and the wail of sirens sounded down the road as Bunny entered the autopsy suite holding a brown paper bag that was sealed with red tape. "Dr. Washburn, I opened this to see what it was. I think the handbag inside belongs to Mrs. Murphy."

Only fifteen minutes had passed since the patient formerly assumed to be a corpse had called out to Claire's team for help.

"Leave the bag here," Claire said. "Right now, I'm calling the cops."

As Bunny did as she was told, Claire saw Cindy eyeing the large paper bag on the stretcher recently vacated by Mrs. Murphy.

Without any discernible hesitation, Cindy opened it up and peered inside. Then she pulled out a handsome red leather handbag, opened it, and began laying its contents on the stretcher.

Claire said, "Cindy. What the hell are you doing?"

"I'm just taking a quick peek. It's in my nature. I'm an investigative reporter, remember?"

Claire said, "Thanks for the news flash. Listen to me. I disavow all knowledge of what you're doing. You know full well the contents of that bag are off-limits and off the record. By tampering with them, you could mess up a case against the shooter. Do you hear me?"

But Cindy took Claire's disavowal as a yellow light, not a red one. She listed the contents of the bag out loud as she emptied the capacious interior and the many pockets. "Here's her wallet, Claire. The driver's license belongs to our not-actually-departed Joan, and the picture matches the woman we just met. She lives on El Camino Del Mar in Seacliff. She has five credit cards in here and a buncha receipts.

"Wow. Look at her makeup kit, Claire. I've seen ads for this stuff. The makeup is infused with stem cells tailored to your own DNA. Well, so they say, anyway. I, on the other hand, say it's expensive. Lots of brushes and sponges, and okay, enough with the makeup.

"She's also got a photo in the glassine sleeve behind the driver's license. It's a picture of Joan and a man who could be her husband."

Cindy let out a low whistle. "This man is handsome."

Then she flipped the plastic sleeve over and read the inscription, "Robert and me, Cannes, second honeymoon, 2016."

Robert appeared to be ten years younger than Joan, at least. He was very good-looking. Dark hair, tall and built, a definite ten. He looked like Tom Selleck when he was Magnum, PI.

Cindy said, "Claire, look at this picture of Joan and her husband, Robert."

"Nope. You're going to get us in trouble with the law."

Cindy said, "I'm wearing gloves. Look." She wiggled her fingers.

"No harm done, Claire. Okay, I've been through everything, every pocket and every secret zippered section. A woman with a four-thousand-dollar handbag would have jewelry, but Joan wasn't wearing any jewelry and there wasn't a single piece in her bag, either. But look at what she's wearing in the photo. Diamonds on her fingers, encircling both wrists, and draped around her throat. That pendant alone has to be eight carats. Maybe even bigger."

"Hey, Girl Reporter," Claire said, "put it all back like you found it. Seal the paper bag. I'm going to wash my hands. Be back in two minutes."

"Got it."

Claire went into the kitchenette and picked up the notes from last night's intake that Dr. H. had left her. She ran her finger down the list of deceased. There were the three car-crash victims. Two on the list were checked off with appended death certificates. Dr. H. had also listed the two who came in after them.

Female, Joan Murphy. Male, John Doe.

Two people had been brought in by the van at the same time. John Doe was in the drawer next to Joan Murphy.

Dr. H. had done a cursory external exam and had written notes:

White female, 45, Joan Murphy, non-fatal gunshot to right shoulder. Flesh wound on hip. COD, pending. John Doe, white male, approx. age 35-40, two shots to the back and one to the left arm. COD, gunshot to the heart. MOD, homicide.

Claire closed the folder and dropped it off in her office. Then she returned to the autopsy suite where Cindy was replacing the tape on the bag of Joan Murphy's possessions.

Claire said, "Cin, as much as I love you, you really have to go. I've got work to do, and honestly, you can't know any of this until next of kin is notified and we've got a green light for speaking to the press."

"I understand. I'm outta here," Cindy said. "I'll talk to you later."

Claire was about to open John Doe's drawer when Greg, the receptionist, called out to her from the front desk.

"Dr. Washburn. Inspector Richard Conklin called. He said to tell you that he wants to see the John Doe."

"Call him back and tell him that now is fine."

CHAPTER 7

WHEN RICH CONKLIN WOKE up earlier that morning, he reached for Cindy—but her side of the bed was empty. And it wasn't even warm anymore.

It took him a few minutes to remember that she was dog-sitting for Lindsay. He smiled. It had been sweet of her not to wake him up.

Rich got moving. He showered, dressed, ate buttered toast over the sink, and washed it down with a Yoo-hoo. He started up his old Bronco on the first try and then made the drive to the Hall of Justice, where he worked in the Southern Station, Homicide Division. He was parking his car a block away from the Hall on Harriet Street when he got a call from Claire. She filled him in on the bizarre happenings in her office.

"I'll punch in at work and get back to you," he said.

It was eight thirty when Conklin entered the squad room. Lieutenant Jackson Brady was inside his office, which was located at the back corner of the bullpen. Conklin crossed the room and knocked on the glass office door. Brady waved him in.

Brady was a veteran of Miami vice and homicide, and had taken over the command of this squad when Warren Jacobi moved up to chief. Conklin thought that in some ways, it was a waste of talent to keep Brady behind the desk, but he was an excellent CO. He was direct, smart, and unafraid. Brady was also Rich's friend, but during work hours, he was all business.

Conklin took a chair opposite Brady and said, "Lieu, I got a call from the ME. Two bodies came in last night. Both had gunshot wounds. One of them is a John Doe. The other is a female who resumed breathing and started talking while she was inside the body bag."

"Christ. What did you just say? The female victim wasn't really dead? Did I hear that correctly?"

"Yup. Her name is Joan Murphy and she's on the way to Saint Francis. I'd like to be on the case."

Brady said, "Let me see who caught it last night."

Conklin looked out the window, watching the traffic on the freeway as Brady's fingers tapped on the keyboard.

"Okay. Okay," Brady said. "Summing it up here, it seems like it was a madhouse in the morgue last night. There was a car crash with three fatalities. Then, this case came in. It started with a 911 call from the Warwick Hotel. A housekeeper went into room 321 to turn down the bed and found two dead bodies in it."

Conklin muttered, "Holy shit."

Brady continued his summary.

"Sergeant Chi got a search warrant and met Detectives Sackowitz and Linden at the hotel. Room three twenty-one was registered to Joan Murphy, who lives locally, over in Seacliff. Murphy's body was completely naked on the bed. She had a gunshot wound to the right shoulder and another that had grazed her hip. She was covered with blood and had no detectable vital signs. Hear that, Conklin? Not breathing. No heartbeat."

"Unreal," said Conklin. "Keep going."

Brady said, "Continuing. The male victim is in the morgue and isn't talking or breathing. He's white, in his thirties, and was also found naked and lying on top of the female. There was no wallet, no ID to be found. He was wearing a wedding band. The male vic took three shots, two to the back, one in the left arm. The murder weapon wasn't found."

Brady took a slug of coffee and then went on.

"Sackowitz and Linden waited for the wagon to arrive. ME techs pronounced both victims DOA. Sac and Linden started a canvass in the hotel. They'll look at surveillance video and do the interviews, et cetera, but I agree with you that they could use help."

Conklin said, "Good to hear that. My desk is clean, Brady. Use me."

Brady said, "I don't have anyone free to partner up with you."

"It's just for a few days, Lieu."

Brady said, "Should be okay, I'm thinkin', since Joan Murphy can probably ID the doer. I'm betting the shooter was the wife of the John Doe. Stay on Murphy and get her story."

Brady lifted his icy blue eyes from the computer and turned them on Conklin.

"We're going to need you to use your famous charm when

you interview Miss Murphy, Conklin. This is a sticky situation. We don't want her to sue the city for taking her to the morgue before her time."

"I'll do my best."

Conklin went back to his desk and downloaded the notes from Sac and Linden. Then he called Claire's office, leaving a message with her receptionist.

He said, "Greg, tell Dr. Washburn I'm on the case. I want to see the John Doe, ASAP."

CHAPTER 8

CONKLIN MADE THE SHORT walk from the back exit from the Hall of Justice lobby, along the breezeway to the ME's office in under two minutes. He was thinking about this murky case of a dead woman who was not actually dead, and a John Doe who was gunned down in flagrante delicto.

Conklin reviewed Sackowitz's case notes one more time. He'd written that no weapon had been found at the scene of the crime and that the John Doe's wallet was missing. He and Linden were still working the hotel angle, trying to get an ID on the dead man.

If they could figure out who the John Doe was, they might be able to learn why he was shot in the first place.

Was the John Doe the target? That would make Joan Murphy a victim of circumstance. And why hadn't the shooter finished off Joan Murphy? She had witnessed the crime, after all. Had the shooter assumed that she was dead?

Could be.

According to the reports, she'd been covered with blood, both hers and the John Doe's. Her muscles had gone rigid. Her breathing and pulse had hardly been there, and were so delicate that they'd become undetectable. Apparently, neither the cops nor the ME techs had ever seen anything like this before, and Murphy's deathlike state had fooled them all. How scary was that?

Conklin pulled open the double glass doors to the ME's office as another question popped into his head. Why hadn't anyone heard the shots?

But he shook his head, clearing out his mind. There were several people waiting in the reception area to see Claire: some were cops, others legal aides and administrators who worked at the Hall. He needed to get control of this situation before it got out of hand.

The receptionist knew Conklin, so as soon as he saw him he said, "She's waiting for you, Inspector. Go on in."

Conklin knew his way around the ME's office and took the main corridor, which led to the autopsy suite in the back.

Claire was gowned and masked. Her assistants were backing her up as she worked on the postmortem assessment of a young boy with a visible head injury. She saw Conklin come in and covered the child with a sheet. Then she shucked her gloves and put on a clean pair. She picked up a large brown paper bag from an empty table and said, "Let's go into my office, Richie."

As he stood with her in her office, Conklin watched Claire open the paper bag on her desk and take out the large, blood-red leather handbag with what looked to be expensive stitching and details.

Claire said, "This purse belongs to Joan. I also have bags of her clothes and those belonging to the John Doe. But let's look at the contents of her handbag first."

She began taking items out of the handbag. There was a nice-looking wallet, a makeup case, keys, and an assortment of other commonplace items.

"This is a pricey bag," Claire told Conklin. "It appears that Mrs. Murphy is a woman of means."

She handed over the wallet. Conklin opened it and looked through the contents.

Claire said, "Look at this."

She was pointing to a photograph under plastic of a man and woman at a resort, their backs to the ocean. Claire flipped the sleeve over, and Conklin read the inscription. "Robert and Me, Cannes, Second Honeymoon, 2016."

Claire said, "Notice the necklace Joan is wearing in the photograph. That pendant is a helluva big diamond. There is a similar enormous rock in her engagement ring, and the wedding band is encrusted with other precious stones. Look at all the glittering bangle bracelets. Joan clearly likes her diamonds."

"A girl's best friend, right?"

"That's what they say. But, Richie, no jewelry was found on her person or in her bag."

"She was robbed."

"That's my first guess."

Conklin made notes, then said, "What do you say, Claire? Can you introduce me to Mr. Doe?"

"I'm dying to meet the man myself," said Claire.

They walked back to the autopsy suite and Claire pulled open the drawer next to the one that had been vacated recently by Joan Murphy.

Conklin found the unknown man to be as described. He was a white male who seemed to be in his thirties. He had a slight paunch and a lot of chest hair. From his conservative haircut and manicure, Conklin guessed that the guy was some sort of businessman. He looked like he could be a sales executive of some sort.

Conklin told Claire what Sackowitz had put in his case notes. "He was found naked, lying on the naked body of Mrs. Murphy."

Claire said, "That seems right. Looks to me like he took the first two shots to his back. Then, he probably turned to face the shooter and that's when he got this one to the underside of his biceps. It went through the muscle and into the chest. That could have been the slug that stopped his heart forever."

Conklin said, "So, who do we think was the shooter? Mrs. Doe? Did she get someone to let her into the room so she could kill her husband? It's a logical explanation. An obvious one. Or could it have been Mr. Murphy, who killed the man cuckolding him? Is that why his wife was spared?

"And if the motive was a domestic beef," Conklin continued, "why take the jewelry? Was it staging, to make the shooting look like a robbery?"

Claire listened as Conklin continued theorizing out loud. He said, "Or was it, in fact, a robbery? A stranger gets into the room or he was waiting in the room. He gets the loot and John Doe's wallet. But why didn't he give Mrs. Murphy a shot to the head so she couldn't testify? Was he convinced she was dead?"

Claire cut off his musings, saying, "Here's my theory. Anyone would have been convinced that that woman, Joan Murphy, died in that hotel room. You see, there's an unusual condition called 'catalepsy.' If this is that condition, it's my first experience with it. I know that death is a many-part process. Different parts of the body cease at different times. Skin lives for twenty-four hours after a person dies, for instance.

"So, catalepsy is a nervous condition that looks like death even though it's an attenuated slow-down. If Mrs. Murphy had not been refrigerated overnight, she would have suffered brain death and she would have died."

"Okay, so what causes catalepsy?"

"Could be a number of things. Parkinson's disease, epilepsy, cocaine withdrawal. It can be a side effect of an antipsychotic. And one of the most common causes can be traumatic shock."

Conklin said, "She had to be pretty traumatized, all right. You think her memory will ever come back?"

Claire shrugged and said, "It's possible. Let me know, will you? I can't really explain it, but I feel somewhat attached to Joan. I want to know what happened to her and why."

CHAPTER 9

CONKLIN CAME THROUGH THE gate to the Homicide squad room and went directly to the small island made up of two facing desks—his and Lindsay's—and a side chair.

He grabbed his desk phone and called St. Francis Memorial. He was shunted around to various bureaucrats until finally a head nurse told him that Mrs. Murphy was in stable condition and was currently having a CAT scan.

Conklin said he'd call back. He was glad to have time to do a background check on the miraculous Mrs. Murphy before meeting with her.

He booted up his computer and began opening the databases that were at his disposal at the police office. He learned that Joan Murphy, nee Tuttle, had been born in New York in 1972. Her mother had been an editor at a high-fashion magazine and her father was CEO of a business machine corporation. Joan had gone to private schools and had capped off her high school diploma with a degree in literature from Berkeley.

Murphy's first husband, Jared Knowles, was a well-regarded art director in Hollywood. Her second and current husband,

Robert Murphy, was a model and small-time actor who was born in 1986. Conklin did the quick math in his head. That made Robert fourteen years younger than his wife.

Joan had bought and paid for the Murphys' home prior to her marriage to Robert, and it had since been featured in multiple glossy style magazines. The Murphys were also pictured in many of the society columns and had a handful of celebrity friends. On the face of it, they seemed to have a pretty good quality of life.

Conklin stretched, taking a break. He texted Sackowitz, telling him he was going to interview Joan Murphy ASAP. After that, he scavenged the refrigerator in the break room and found a container of yogurt marked "Boxer." He grabbed the snack, knowing Lindsay wouldn't mind.

He ate at his desk and opened the criminal databases, finding zip, zero, and nada on Joan and Robert Murphy. They hadn't ever been in trouble with the law. No scandals, no shoplifting, no nothing.

Next, Conklin looked at all online photos he could find of this nice, upscale couple. What had happened to Joan? She seemed to have a decent life, but then one night she checks into a hotel room and entertains a man who isn't her husband. A shooter somehow gets into this hotel room and blows away the lover. Then that same assassin wings the millionairess and leaves her for dead.

And what had happened to Joan's jewelry? Had the whole thing been a pre-planned armed robbery? It was starting to look that way to Conklin. Maybe it hadn't been about the duplicitous relationship after all.

Suddenly, his desk phone rang, jerking him out of his thoughts.

The caller ID read SACKOWITZ.

"It's crazy that Joan Murphy is alive, right?" he said to the night-shift detective.

Sac said, "My thinking exactly. Who's the target here? Or was this a robbery that got out of control?"

Conklin said, "I've been wondering the same thing. Hopefully this interview helps us figure things out. Then, after I see Mrs. Murphy, I'm going to drive out to her home so I can talk to the husband. I'll let you know how it goes."

"Sounds like a plan. But be careful."

PRESENT TIME

CHAPTER 10

RICH CONKLIN HAD FINISHED his useless bedside interview with Joan Murphy, but before they could go to Claire Washburn's office, Joan had to be cleared to leave the hospital.

He called Cindy from the waiting room and left her a voice mail telling her that she shouldn't hold dinner for him. Minutes later, the attending physician came down the hallway to ask him to come with him to his patient's room.

Once he was standing at Joan's side, Dr. Kornacki turned to Conklin and said, "I want you to be my witness on this situation. I told Mrs. Murphy she should stay with us overnight, so that we could keep an eye on her for twenty-four hours at minimum."

Joan chirped, "And I said, 'No thanks, doctor. I'm fine now.' And I really, truly am. I'm ready to go home."

Kornacki said sternly, "There's a chance that you might relapse if you leave, but I can't force you to stay here. See your regular physician. Please do it tomorrow."

Joan plucked at the hospital-issue nightgown. "Detective, may I please have my clothing and other belongings back? I must have been wearing quite a bit of jewelry. I'm never without my engagement ring and mother's necklace."

Conklin ran his hand down the side of his face. "Unfortunately, Joan, we weren't able to locate your jewelry. And your clothing will need to stay with our team for now, for testing."

Joan sighed and said, "Doctor, may I borrow some scrubs? Either blue or green would be fine with me."

Conklin stood outside as Joan dressed and then he co-signed the "Against Medical Advice" release form. He watched as Joan submitted to the nurses, who were fussing around her as they seated her in a wheelchair.

He pushed Joan's chair out to his car. The foot well on the passenger side was filled with litter, and Joan sniffed in disgust when she saw it.

"Sorry," he said. "I can get that."

He gathered up the pile of fast-food wrappers and empty water bottles, and then placed it on the seat of the wheelchair. He walked the trash over to a garbage receptacle and returned the chair to the lobby.

He'd rarely worked a case as incomprehensible as this double homicide that only had one actual fatality. But he was determined to see it through to its conclusion. Whatever that might be.

When he and Joan were both in the car and buckled up, she said, "Richard, why not just drop me at home? We can shake hands and say good-bye. I'll write a note to your superior saying how good you have been to me. You have been very nice."

"Joan, there was a dead body of a man found in a bed with you. He has a family out there somewhere and they're never going to see him again. Someone killed him." He wanted to add, *Does that ring a bell?* but he bit down on the sarcasm. The last thing he wanted to do was drive his witness underground.

Joan said nothing in reply. She just looked out the window at rush hour traffic on Pine.

He continued, "We're going to make a quick stop at the medical examiner's office. Twenty minutes after that, you'll be home."

She said, "I know I said I would look at that man. But this isn't easy for me, Richard. I have really bad memories of that place."

"I know you do. But can you try to look at this a different way? Your unscheduled stop at the ME's office was a blip in the span of your life. Now you're alive and well, and you're helping out the San Francisco Police Department. For about two minutes, you're going to return to the site of a personal miracle."

She looked at him dubiously.

Rich gave her one of his beautiful smiles and said, "I'm not going to leave your side. You want the sirens, Joan? Or shall we just enjoy the ride?"

She let out a good laugh.

"Sirens," she said.

Conklin grinned at her.

He flipped on the sirens and the lights, and they headed

toward the medical examiner's office. He couldn't wait to reintroduce Joan to Mr. John Doe. He had absolutely no idea—couldn't even guess—what she would say or do when she looked at the man's dead body.

But he had a feeling her reaction was going to surprise him.

CHAPTER 11

CONKLIN DRAPED HIS WINDBREAKER around Joan Murphy's narrow shoulders and walked her from Harriet Street to the ME's office.

Claire was waiting for them at the open rear door. She gently placed her arm around Joan and told her how glad she was to see her.

"How's that shoulder? Are you feeling okay?" Claire asked.

"The pain pills are telling me that I feel just fine." Joan Murphy's smile faded as she looked around the autopsy suite. She stiffly walked with Claire and Richie into the cool room in the back. There, she took in the sight of the stacked stainless-steel drawers that were holding bodies of the dead.

Claire said cautiously, "Are you ready, Joan? I'm going to open the drawer now."

Joan Murphy shook her head and said, "I'm never going to be ready for this. But let's get it over with."

Claire slid the drawer open slowly. Wisps of brown hair peeked out over the top of the crisp sheet, followed by a long topographical stretch of white. The sight before them terminated with a man's knobby toes.

Claire carefully folded the sheet down below John Doe's chin.

Conklin stood beside Joan as she peered down at the dead man's blanched and chubby face. To Rich, the man's features were unremarkable. He looked like a typical suburban dad, the kind of guy who would watch out for the kids on the block, was handy around the house, and didn't fool around at the office.

Clearly, his appearance didn't square with the circumstances in which his body had been discovered.

Joan stared at the corpse for a long moment. Then she seemed almost indignant when she said, "I'm supposed to know this person?"

Conklin looked past Joan to Claire. Their eyes met. He said, "Joan, this is the man who was found dead, naked, and in bed with you in room three twenty-one at the Warwick. His wallet was stolen. We're trying to identify him and it's only a matter of time before we're successful. And we could do it faster and better if you can give us a name or a lead."

"Sorry to disappoint, Richard. I've never seen this man before, and honestly, I don't think I would even notice him if he walked by me on the street. He's not my type.

"Here's my theory," she continued, looking up at Conklin. "Somehow, both he and I were drugged, kidnapped, put into that bed, and shot. Maybe he was already dead. I was as good as dead, and maybe they didn't realize that I was still kicking. There's no other explanation."

Conklin stifled a laugh. He couldn't believe that Joan had

come up with the fantastic theory that somehow two people had been kidnapped and smuggled into the Warwick, where they were stripped, posed, and shot, in that order. For what purpose? To create a scandal?

Maybe to create a pulp fiction murder tableau for a book cover.

He arranged his features in a straight face. "But why would anyone do that to you?"

"How would I know? I don't have a criminal mind. And now, I'm ready to go home. Didn't you hear the doctor? I need to rest."

CHAPTER 12

CONKLIN HAD PROMISED TO bring Joan home and he kept his word. He walked her back to his car and drove them to Seacliff. The sun was going down and house lights winked on along Lake Street. Conklin turned right on 28th and took it to El Camino Del Mar. When he pulled into her neighborhood, he noticed that it was an upmarket, oceanside area dotted with large estates. Many of them had water views and private access to the shoreline. Joan was looking straight ahead, saying to him, "How am I going to explain all of this to Robert?"

"That you were found in bed with another man?"

"What? No. He'll believe me when I say that I was drugged and kidnapped. But I have to explain getting shot. Why would anyone shoot me? Maybe Robert got a call from the kidnapper. Maybe he had to pay ransom money or something. Did you think of that, Richard?"

Joan had some pretty crazy theories about her attempted murder, but this time, she had a point. Her husband hadn't reported his wife as missing. Could he have forked over a ransom payment while he was waiting for his wife's return?

Rich Conklin couldn't wait to see Robert Murphy's face when Joan came through the front door to her house—alive.

Maybe it would give him the final clue to crack this case.

CHAPTER 13

THE CLOSER THEY CAME to Joan's home on El Camino Del Mar, the more anxious Joan became. She tried to call her husband again, as Mallory had done when Joan had first woken up in the morgue, but the call went unanswered.

"I'm very frightened now," Joan said to Conklin. "What if we find him shot and lying dead on the floor? What if my kidnapping was part of a larger plot?"

"Everything's going to be okay, Joan. We'll investigate every piece of evidence we find. If a clue surfaces in your memory, you know where to reach me."

The brass house numbers were embedded in the gateposts that flanked the driveway leading to a handsome Mediterranean-style stucco house with a tiled roof. The gate was open, revealing manicured gardens inside the walls. Conklin pulled his car up the long driveway and parked it between a blue Mercedes XL sedan and a silver Bentley.

"Which one is Robert's car?" he asked Joan.

"The Mercedes. The Bentley is mine."

Conklin went around to the passenger side and helped Joan out of the car. He retrieved her handbag from the foot well and held it open for her while she searched inside it for her keys. When she found them, she handed the set to him.

They reached the front door, and Conklin unlocked it. He pushed the door open and said, "Stay here. I'll go in first to make sure everything is safe."

Conklin took three steps into the room, entering the foyer. Lights were on inside the house, but the security alarms weren't set.

He called out, "Mr. Murphy? This is the SFPD."

There was no answer. Conklin drew his gun and held it out, but he kept the muzzle pointing down. He walked through the foyer, which emptied into a spacious living area decorated with modern furnishings. The windows along the far wall looked out over lawns with topiary and a small pathway of stone steps. A large swimming pool was across the lawn and off to the right.

He called Mr. Murphy's name again as he rounded a corner. He heard music coming from outside the sliding glass doors, where a set of teak outdoor furniture faced the ocean.

A man stood up and turned to Conklin, holding a sheaf of paper in his hand. He was big, not just tall, but well-built and handsome. He was wearing what looked to be a cashmere half-zip sweater and expensive jeans. He showed no sign of injury.

Conklin said, "Mr. Murphy?"

The man said, "Who the hell are you? And how did you get into my house?"

"I'm Inspector Conklin, SFPD. I've brought your wife home from the hospital."

"Oh? I didn't know. Why was Joan in the hospital?"

"She was shot, Mr. Murphy. Let me go get her. I'll tell her that you're back here."

Conklin went back out to the front door and told Joan Murphy that her husband seemed fine. She smiled and then started to weep. Conklin holstered his gun and accompanied the frail woman, who was still wearing blue scrubs, paper slides, and an SFPD windbreaker.

When he saw Joan, her husband opened his arms and folded her in. He patted her back as she sobbed against his chest.

"I almost died, Robert. I almost died."

Conklin thought that Murphy's actions were warm, but his expression and his affect seemed to be a little distant. Conklin watched and listened as Joan gave Robert a shorthand version of the story as she knew it. *But why didn't Joan's husband seem shocked by the news?*

Joan told Robert that she had woken up in the morgue. Apparently she had been shot in the shoulder and had a wound on her hip as well, but she had no memory of being attacked. Thank goodness she had no broken bones. She just needed some TLC and rest.

There was no mention of the deceased John Doe.

Robert asked her where this had happened and she said, "At the Warwick, Robert. I was found in a hotel room, bloody and unconscious. The police thought I was dead! My jewelry was gone. That lovely pendant of my mother's. And oh, my God. My rings were taken, too."

"Why were you at the Warwick?"

"I have no idea how I got there, Robbie. I think that I was drugged and kidnapped."

"Drugged and kidnapped? My God, Joan. By whom?"

"That's my theory, but this kind man, Inspector Conklin, is going to figure out what happened and who is responsible."

"God, I hope so," Robert said as he hugged her close one more time. "We're going to take good care of you, dear."

From inside his embrace, Joan looked up at her husband and smiled.

"I'm going to change into my own comfortable clothes, Robert. I could use a drink. Tell Marjorie I'm very hungry. I have no idea when I last had a meal. I think I'd like chicken stew. That will fix me right up. Inspector, you're welcome to stay for dinner. I'll be right back."

When Joan had left the room, Conklin turned to Robert Murphy and said, "You mind answering a few questions for me?"

CHAPTER 14

MURPHY NODDED HIS HEAD and directed Conklin to a squared, taupe-colored chair. As Conklin sat down, Murphy took a seat in an identical chair that was situated at a right angle from him. Murphy did finger riffs on his knees, looking impatient and resigned.

Conklin said, "These are routine questions, Mr. Murphy. Your wife was shot and left for dead. So I'm going to need details of your movements over the last forty-eight hours."

Murphy said, "Right. I know this one. You think the husband did it."

Conklin said, "Not necessarily. Think of this as the way we clear the husband, Mr. Murphy."

Murphy sighed, raked back his hair with his fingers, and said, "I didn't leave the property all weekend and I haven't left it today, either. Marjorie Bright, our housekeeper and cook, can vouch for me. Our pool boy, Peter Carter, saw me Sunday morning when I went for a swim. Gotta stay fit, no? Peter lives in a cottage in the back. He has the weekends off, but he was there on Sunday."

Conklin said, "You seriously haven't left the house in two whole days?"

"Honestly, it's been longer than that. I have a part in a movie. It's a thriller called *Case Management*. Craig Noble is directing and I play Evan Slaughter, the lead detective. I've been reading and rehearsing my lines for these past couple days. Marjorie even helped me run through them. She usually does. Anyway, we start shooting next week."

Conklin asked, "Were you contacted by anyone demanding ransom for Joan's return?"

"What? No. Of course not. I would have called the police if that had happened."

Conklin said, "Can you think of any reason why someone might want to hurt Joan?"

"I doubt it. But she does have a strong personality. She always says what she thinks. She's on a lot of committees and charity boards. Wherever money and politics are involved, people can get pretty pissed off. Thankfully, Joan keeps me out of her business."

Conklin nodded, wondering, *Does this actor really think that murders spring from charity board decisions?* Both Joan and Robert had B-movie theories to real-life murder. It was just another clue that they might be hiding something.

Rich said, "Mr. Murphy, when your wife didn't come home Sunday night, weren't you worried about her?"

"As I said, Joan does what Joan wants to do. We don't question each other, Inspector. And if your next question is 'Do you love your wife?' the answer is 'I like her independence, her humor, and her intelligence.' And yes, I do love her as well."

"I have to ask you. Do you think your wife could be having an affair?"

Murphy gave Conklin a scathing look and said, "If she is having an affair, it would shock the hell out of me. We have a full and trusting relationship. Thank you for bringing her home safely. I'd like daily reports on your progress in finding the kidnapper."

Joan Murphy returned to the room in flowing garments, looking like an entirely different woman. She was relaxed. Beaming. Confident.

"Richard," she said. "You'll have dinner with us, right?"

"I wish I could, Joan. Maybe another time. But before I leave, I need a few moments with Marjorie."

CHAPTER 15

JOAN BROUGHT CONKLIN TO the kitchen, where he met with Marjorie Bright, a wiry, blue-eyed woman who was about sixty years old. She was dressed casually in dark pants and an untucked white shirt.

She dried her hands on a dish towel and checked on the contents of the oven. After Joan had left the room, she and Conklin sat down at the kitchen table.

Conklin asked some preliminary questions. How long had she worked for the Murphys? What did she think of them? Had she ever witnessed any arguments between the two of them?

Miss Bright told Conklin that she had worked for Miss Joan for thirteen years. She lived in a private suite on the third floor. She seemed happy with her job in the Murphys' home.

When Conklin asked if the couple fought, she shrugged and said, "I guess there's been some shouting over the last five years, but there's never been any violence. They have separate suites connected by a hallway on the second floor. Their lives are separate, mostly, but sometimes they'll entertain at home, vacation, and attend functions together. They live well in this house, and I do think they are in love."

Conklin asked, "Do you recall if Mr. Murphy was home on Sunday?"

"Yes, he was here. I'm off on Sundays, but my rooms overlook the front of the property and his car never moved. I saw him and Joan eating breakfast together on the patio on Sunday morning. Later that afternoon, Mr. Robert called up and asked if I could help him rehearse his lines. He's very talented, you know."

"Could you estimate the time that Mrs. Murphy left the house on Sunday?"

"No. Like I said, it was my day off, so I wasn't looking at the clock. Besides, she doesn't like to drive. She usually uses a car service, so I couldn't guess a time for you, since her car never left the driveway."

The housekeeper got the name and number of the service, and after Conklin thanked her, he returned to the sprawling drawing room and told the Murphys he'd be in touch as soon as his team had any kind of big break or lead in the case.

Once he got in the car, he called Cindy and talked to her as he drove home. They clicked off when Rich was on Kirkham with his apartment building in sight, and that's when his phone rang with another call.

It was Sackowitz.

"We've got an ID on our John Doe," Sac said. "His name's Samuel J. Alton and he's from San Bernardino. He's the senior VP in claims for Avantra Insurance. He's married, has three kids under twelve, and is a regular at the Warwick Hotel. On the first Sunday of every month, he comes to town for a Monday morning meeting at Avantra's main office on Beale Street."

"Interesting," said Conklin. "What are you thinking? Was Alton Joan's boyfriend? An attacker? A random hookup?"

"I'm going with boyfriend. We were able to get a look into the Warwick computer systems, and it turns out that Joan Murphy has a monthly reservation at the Warwick. And it's always on a Sunday night. The first Sunday in the month, in fact."

Conklin said, "I've got to agree with you then. Sounds like these two were having an ongoing affair. Yet Joan's husband tells me there's no chance in hell that his wife is stepping out on him. 'We have a full and trusting relationship,' he told me. And that's a direct quote."

"Gee," said Sac. "Could the husband be telling you a lie?"

Conklin laughed.

Sac said, "I'm going to drive to San Berdoo. I'll notify Mrs. Alton that her husband was shot to death in the arms of another woman. Then, I'm gonna go home and get drunk because that's going to be one hell of a conversation. You want to mention Samuel Alton's name to Joan Murphy? See what happens?"

"Oh, yeah, I do. The woman tells a fantastic story. Can't wait to hear what she comes up with this time."

CHAPTER 16

CINDY WAS AT LINDSAY and Joe's apartment Tuesday morning, drying Martha after their walk had gotten drowned out by an unexpected drenching rain.

Martha shook herself off, causing Cindy to shriek, "No!"

Martha, excited by her friend's response, put her paws on Cindy's shoulders and licked her face.

Cindy couldn't help laughing. Martha was showing good progress with her injury if she was already this mobile. That made Cindy pretty proud to have helped out her friend in need.

"What now, Miss Martha?" she lovingly asked the dog. "Are both of us going to have to get into a hot shower? Hmmmm? You know I have to wear these clothes to work."

Martha woofed. Cindy laughed again and said, "Copy that, Big Girl. Breakfast is coming right up."

Cindy was dumping dog food into a bowl when, of course, the phone rang. It was just like the other morning, only this time it really was Lindsay.

"Are you checking up on me?" Cindy teased.

"Of course not. Well, maybe I am, but just a little. Put Martha on the phone for me."

"Sure thing. Here ya go."

Cindy put the receiver near Martha's face as the dog gobbled down her beef stew with supplements. She could hear Lindsay talking to her dog, who stopped eating long enough to lick the phone. Cindy cracked up.

"I'm totally grossed out," she said to Lindsay. "By the way, it's not just raining here, it's a certified downpour. Your dog is wet. The phone is wet. I'm wet. And I'm about to rifle through your closet so I don't have to go to work in an outfit that's completely soaked."

Lindsay told her, "Go ahead. Be my guest. And take a selfie so I can see how my size ten clothing fits your itty-bitty size-four bod."

"Great idea. So, how's the vacation going?"

Lindsay's voice was as light as fluffy clouds in a blue sky. She told Cindy about their lovely room, the pleasure of "waking up with Joe and not having one damned thing to do. I'm eating actual meals at real tables."

Cindy laughed. "That's amazing. Take a selfie of that."

Lindsay asked if she was missing anything back home, and Cindy had the Joan Murphy story racked up and ready to roll. But at the last second, she held it back. Lindsay was with her hubby, and their baby was with Lindsay's sister. For the first time in a while, her friends were enjoying a nice hotel and room service. Lindsay deserved a clean break while she was on vacation.

"As far as I can tell, life goes on without you, Linds."

Lindsay laughed. Then she promptly told her to shut up and informed her friend that she was going back to bed.

They exchanged love-yous and hung up, and then Cindy picked up where she left off with her chores. It was funny how, even though she had known Martha forever, she felt her feelings toward the fluffy dog had deepened while taking care of her. This doggy was changing from just a typical cute dog to a close friend.

Cindy had been fighting Richie on the subject of having kids for a couple of years now. She wasn't ready for them. Yet he'd been ready since before he'd even met Cindy. At one point, the two of them had actually broken up over this very issue. Thank God they had been able to get past their differences and get back together.

Even though Cindy hadn't changed her position.

Still, being responsible for this old dog made Cindy think she might have some tiny maternal instinct inside her after all.

She threw the wet towels into the wash, left her shoes in the bathtub, and found a pair of Lindsay's sneakers in her closet. They were big, but they almost fit her. Then she dried her hair, and when her blond curls had sprung back into shape, she located a trench coat with a belt in the back of Lindsay's closet. She tried it on and decided it would work well enough.

Before she left the apartment, she called the girls and put them on a conference call.

"Lunch, anyone?"

Claire and Yuki were both in.

CHAPTER 17

CLAIRE STRIPPED OFF HER gown, mask, and gloves. She told her crew that she was going out for a quick lunch and that she would be back in an hour.

MacBain's, the bar and grill down the street from the Hall, was named for a heroic captain of the SFPD who was now deceased. His daughter, Sydney, owned the local watering hole. It specialized in a five-dollar burger-and-fries lunch and was generally packed from twelve noon to midnight with Hall of Justice workers.

Claire, Lindsay, and Yuki were card-carrying customers.

Cindy didn't work at the Hall but had her own card. It said Press on it, and Sydney MacBain was happy to have her business.

At a quarter past noon, the line of customers was trailing out the door, of course. Claire joined it and was greeted moments later by Yuki. The two friends grabbed each other into a big hug.

Yuki had just returned to the DA's office after a year of doing pro bono defense work and was charged up to be putting bad guys away. She had just lost a case of national and global proportions, and was eager to put it behind her by diving into the next one. And Claire had no doubt that her friend would do a phenomenal job on it.

Yuki said, "Tell me all about this woman who apparently came back from the dead in your morgue."

"I can only tell you because she's alive," said Claire. "And because Cindy isn't here."

Yuki drew an X over the breast pocket of her suit jacket with a finger, swearing to keep the secret.

So Claire told her. "The subject, who shall remain nameless, was found naked under the naked body of a man who was not her husband. He'd taken a few plugs to the back and one to the arm, and she had been shot a couple times, too. She appeared to be dead, but in fact was cataleptic."

"Is that like catatonic?"

Claire laughed. "Not at all."

Just then, there was a tap on Claire's shoulder.

She turned and was standing face-to-face with Cindy Thomas, the crime reporter. Her springy blond hair bounced and shook as she said, "Don't give me that off-the-record crap. I swear not to run anything until you say it's okay. Okay?"

Yuki said, "I feel like I've heard this pitch before."

The three friends threw their heads back as they laughed. Then the line moved forward and a table opened up inside. When they were settled at their table and had ordered their burgers and sparkling water, Claire told her friends the rest of the information that she knew about the case.

"The unnamed female's outfit was collected from the hotel

room and is with my team, currently undergoing testing. It's a two-piece Givenchy suit, a black button-down shirt, evening slacks, and high-heeled sandals. Also, she had *very* expensive undergarments. The kind that I can only afford in my dreams."

Cindy said to Claire, "You've been holding out on me."

Then she turned to Yuki and said, "So, here's the rest of it— as I was able to figure out." She cracked a sly grin.

"This naked man who was found lying on top of this unnamed female. Let's call her, well, let's call her, Joan—"

Claire shook her head and sighed.

The food arrived at the table, and after the ladies took a few bites, Cindy went on. "The naked man was shot dead and Joan was also hit by a couple of slugs. She appeared to be dead. Stonecold dead. But she was not. And based on the *very* expensive undergarments and the nakedness, it seems like she went to the hotel with recreation in mind."

Yuki said, "So are there any other theories besides the obvious? Do we know for certain that she was having an affair with the John Doe?"

Cindy said, "When I met her, she was just regaining consciousness. She told us that she had completely lost her memory."

"And it could be true," Claire told her friends. "She was out of it for six hours, at least. The refrigeration saved her life, but that's not to say she didn't lose a few memories. She needs a neurological workup and I hope she gets one."

"Or she could be lying," said Yuki. "You say she knew her

name but not what happened to her in that hotel room? That's pretty convenient, if you ask me."

Cindy put down her burger and pointed a French fry at her friend before she dipped it into a puddle of ketchup. "If you met her and talked with her, you'd believe her, Yuki."

"I'm a human lie detector," Yuki said sweetly. "I'll bet if I met her, I still wouldn't believe her. I'm pretty sure she's a very charming and skillful liar."

Claire sighed, looked down at her watch, and said, "I have time for a quick coffee if you do."

When she glanced back up at Cindy's face, she could tell that her friend had disappeared down a road of deep thought.

No doubt she was working on a story headlined "Dead Woman Walking."

CHAPTER 18

RICH CONKLIN WAS AT his desk in the squad room. He was doing a background check on the deceased, since he now had his name.

Samuel J. Alton had a negligible record. Twenty years before, when he was seventeen, he had been busted for selling pot at a beach party in LA. He'd pled guilty to the misdemeanor, got six months' probation, and paid a fine. It seemed he'd learned his lesson, though, because after that he hadn't gotten so much as a parking ticket.

But Sam Alton wasn't exactly a model citizen, because once a month he came to town, stayed at the Warwick, and apparently spent time with a very wealthy woman who had a home in an exclusive part of town. That woman always booked a room for the two of them. She also happened to have a husband. And he'd had a wife and kids.

Had last weekend's tryst gotten Sam Alton killed?

If so, by whom? How did the killer gain access to the room?

And if his death wasn't caused by a scorned spouse, what was the motive for the shooting?

Conklin opened a file of photos. Dr. H. had taken some at the scene, while Claire had taken the others. In Claire's pictures of the victim, he was resting on a metal table in her lab. She'd also included close-ups of the labels. Seeing Claire's careful, meticulous work made Conklin smile. She was very good at her job.

There was a second zip file containing photographs of Sam Alton's clothing that had been stowed away at the hotel.

The attached note from Dr. H. read:

See Joan Murphy's clothes as they were found in the room. No GSR on them. Same deal with John Doe's apparel. The clothing was neatly folded on a chair, jacket hung in the closet. Also no GSR. The lab has it all now and is processing for trace. We'll get who did this.

Rich stared at the pictures for a while. What the neatly hung and folded clothing told him was that these two people knew each other well. He saw no violence, but he didn't see any uncontrollable passion, either. It felt to him as though Joan and Samuel had been a couple for a while. He thought about the way Joan had stared at Alton's dead body.

What had she said? "I've never seen this man before."

And she had seemed indignant.

Her voice had been hard. Cold. Had it been full of guilty knowledge? Had she set Alton up to be killed? Or had she suffered brain damage that had resulted in memory loss while she was in that cataleptic state? Did she truly not remember her lover?

Conklin's cell phone vibrated. He looked at the caller ID and saw that it was Robert Murphy.

Rich answered the phone by simply saying his name, and Joan's husband replied, "This is Robert Murphy. Have you heard from Joan?"

"Not today. Why do you ask?"

"She's missing, Inspector. She slept in her bed last night, but both she and her car are gone now."

"Can you please give me the plate number?"

Murphy recited the numbers.

Conklin asked, "Is there a tracking device on her phone?"

"You've got me there. I don't have the slightest idea. Inspector, I'm worried about her. Especially in light of recent events."

Rich said, "I'll put out a lookout on her car and will let you know if I hear anything. If you hear from her in the meantime, please call me."

"I will."

Conklin hung up and then played the conversation back in his mind. Had Murphy been straight with him or was he acting? It seemed strange that he would be worried that Joan was missing for a few hours, even though he hadn't been ruffled when she'd been missing for almost twenty-four hours.

The alarm bells were going off in Conklin's head. Something just didn't add up.

What had happened to Joan?

Had she collapsed somewhere and gone into another cataleptic state? Had her husband killed her? Or perhaps she'd just gone somewhere to grieve for her dead lover because the memories from the shooting came back.

Whatever the reason, Rich wasn't going to chance it. He called Joan's number and left a message. "Joan, it's Rich Conklin," he said. "Please call me. I'm concerned for your safety."

CHAPTER 19

RICH WAS AT HIS desk when John Sackowitz dropped by and sat down in Lindsay's chair. Sac was a big man and was wearing a gray jacket, jeans, white shirt, and a weird pink tie.

Sac moved the desk lamp out of his way so he could look Conklin directly in the eye. Then he said, "Sam Alton's betrayed widow, Rachel, is in shock. It's nightmare city over at her house. God, I hate notifications. Did you get a chance to speak to Joan?"

"She's gone missing. That's according to her husband anyway. I'm heading out to Seacliff to tour the house and grounds. I'll call you later."

Sac stood up and said, "I've got some paperwork to do." He lumbered over to his desk across the room and began typing up his report.

Conklin turned off his desktop and waved good-bye to Sac.

A few minutes later, he was in his car and driving out to Seacliff when Brady called.

"Conklin, a dead body was found in an apartment building in West Portal. Welky was the first one on the scene, and an

ADA just brought him a search warrant. Welky found two IDs in the room and a wallet that belongs to Samuel J. Alton."

Seriously? There was no way Samuel J. Alton had died twice.

So who was this dead man with his wallet?

Conklin made the excruciatingly slow drive to the middle-class, family-oriented neighborhood. He got stuck at the lights at both the entrance and exit of a three-block shopping district, and then, once he'd gotten free of that, he hit another traffic snarl on a block filled with homey bars and restaurants. Twenty minutes after leaving the Hall, he parked in front of an apartment building on West Portal Avenue, between a cruiser and the coroner's van. He hopped out of his car and headed toward the crime scene.

The building was a classic midcentury San Francisco–style home with five stories of gray stucco, arched windows, and a view of the West Portal Muni. A half dozen trees out front softened the lines of the building under a clear sky overhead. A light-rail car rattled by as Conklin entered the building. If he hadn't been summoned there on police duty, he would have never guessed that there had been a murder inside.

The old man behind the front desk pointed to the elevator behind him, then raised four fingers.

Fourth floor. Got it.

Conklin was met upstairs by the two beat cops who'd arrived on the scene first. Their names were Officers Calvin Welky and Mike Brown. Conklin signed the log, put on booties and gloves, and then walked into a clean, bright three-room apartment.

Welky said, "The manager, Mr. Wayne Murdock, said the apartment belongs to one Arthur O'Brien, an actor and probably a junkie. Murdock got a call from O'Brien's mother. She hadn't heard from her son in a couple of days. She said he wasn't returning her calls. Murdock went to the young man's residence, found his body here, and called it in."

Conklin looked around the living room. It was dominated by a fifty-two-inch TV. Across the room from it sat a nondescript brown couch. A set of weights took up one corner of the space. It looked to Conklin like this was a single man's apartment. There were no knickknacks or sentimental items breaking up the uniform brown color palette. But the most telling detail of all was the drug paraphernalia that was scattered across the coffee table.

Conklin noticed a stubby candle, a scorched spoon, a box of matches, and a flock of opaque glassine envelopes that were coated with white powder.

Conklin walked to the bedroom, stood in the doorway, and nodded to the two CSIs who were photographing the dead man. His body was lying in the center of the unmade bed.

Conklin said hello to Claire and Bunny, and then he took in the whole of the room. There were movie posters on the walls, a laundry bag by the window, a desk with an open laptop computer, and a knapsack up against the wall. His eyes went back to the dead man lying in a relaxed fetal position.

If you squinted, you could almost imagine that Arthur O'Brien was sleeping.

Conklin wished that he could shake the man to ask him some questions.

Who are you, bud? Why do you have Sam Alton's wallet?

CHAPTER 20

CLAIRE WASHBURN PHOTOGRAPHED THE deceased from every angle with her old Minolta camera while she and Bunny waited for Rich Conklin to arrive.

The dead man's real name was Arthur O'Brien. He was white and in his thirties, but since that's where his similarities to Samuel J. Alton ended, it was a wonder that he was in possession of Alton's identification.

Arthur O'Brien didn't have a double chin or love handles. He was as thin as a rail, and had spiky blond hair and a square diamond earring in one ear. He wore jeans and a long-sleeved blue knit shirt. One of his sleeves was rolled up, almost to the shoulder, revealing a length of rubber tubing knotted around his left biceps. The track marks that ran down his arm showed that this had not been his first time at the rodeo. The syringe was lying on the sheets about three inches from his right hand, and there was a puddle of vomit on a pillow.

Probable cause of death: suicide, most likely unintended.

Conklin came through the door. He pushed his hair out of his eyes, then checked out the room and the body. Then he said to her, "Don't commit yourself, but what are your thoughts?"

She said, "I'll send out the blood sample in the morning and do the post, but he's cold. On the face of it, he OD'd and I'd say he's been dead at least twenty-four hours."

Claire lifted up the dead man's shirt and pushed a thermometer into the skin above his liver. Then she waited a minute before reading it.

She said, "I'd estimate that this man's death occurred more than thirty hours ago. That means it happened early Monday morning."

"The wallet's over there," Welky told Conklin, pointing toward the dresser opposite the bed. Conklin walked over, picked it up, and took a look at its contents. Claire had already seen the wallet. It was good quality and was made from tan-colored calf's skin. The initials *SJA* were embossed in one corner.

Inside was Samuel Alton's driver's license. The photo on the identification card matched the face of the man who had been found dead in Joan Murphy's embrace.

"One twenty in cash in the billfold," said Welky, "along with four credit cards and a dozen business cards. Everything seems to belong to Samuel Alton, Avantra Insurance, San Bernardino. Inspector, there's also a backpack you'll want to see here."

Brown picked up the backpack that had been leaning against the wall and set it down on the desk. Claire left the deceased and went over to watch Conklin go through the contents of the bag.

He hefted it, undid the zipper, and said, "Call me crazy, but I'm feeling lucky."

Conklin put his hand into the backpack and removed the first item: a snub-nosed Smith & Wesson, small, what was known as a .38 Special. It held six bullets. He showed Claire the chamber. There was only one bullet left inside.

She thought, *The first three went into Alton's back and arm, and the last two went into Joan Murphy's shoulder and hip. That adds up.*

Conklin handed the weapon off to a CSI, saying, "That goes to ballistics right away, Boyd. It looks like it could be evidence in an active homicide case."

A few more items came out of the backpack, including a bag of chocolate chip cookies and an empty liter-sized Coke bottle with a hole in the bottom. Conklin held up the plastic bottle. He knew that on the street, this sort of thing was used as a suppressor. If a killer screwed the gun into the mouth of the bottle and fired, the bottle would silence the gunshot.

The next item in the bag was a gray T-shirt. Richie sniffed it and said, "Gunpowder."

He handed the shirt and the bottle off to Boyd. Then he put both hands into the bag and took out a red-patterned kerchief that was neatly folded into a bundle. He said, "This is so heavy, it almost feels like it's alive."

Claire saw that the object inside that kerchief was jointed and pointy. Maybe it wasn't one item, but a number of many small pieces wrapped up together. Conklin set the makeshift package down on the desk and turned to Wallace, the CSI who was holding the camera, saying, "Please shoot the hell out of this."

Rich opened the kerchief one fold at a time, exposing a pair of very sparkly earrings, two chunky rings, three diamond encrusted cuff-style bracelets, and a twenty-two-inch white metal chain necklace with a large diamond pendant.

He stared at the glittering array for a long moment. Maybe he was dazzled, thought Claire. Because it was dazzling.

"What do you think of this?" he said to her. "Is it a million dollars' worth of diamonds?"

Claire said, "If it all came from Cartier or Harry Winston, that batch could be worth multiples of that. But I know one thing for sure: those are Joan's jewels. I recognize most of it from that second honeymoon photo that was in her wallet. I'll bet she never expected to see these pieces again."

Conklin dug around in the main section of the backpack some more but came up empty-handed. Then he opened a zippered pocket in the front and took out a wallet. This one was slim, holding only one credit card and a driver's license. He showed Claire the photo on the license. It belonged to the man on the bed, Arthur O'Brien.

Claire said, "There's another pocket on the side there, Richie."

The pocket was tight and the fabric seemed to resist the insertion of his gloved fingers. Conklin persisted. At last, he pulled out a green plastic hotel key card.

He showed it to Claire and put it down on a corner of the desk. He asked Wallace to take a couple of shots of the card. On the center of the card were the words *Warwick Hotel*.

"Beautiful," he said to Claire. "Assuming the gun in the backpack killed Sam Alton, Arthur O'Brien has tied up all the loose ends and wrapped up the case against himself."

Claire nodded curtly as she handed off the pillowcase with the vomit on it. That's when she found the cell phone in the bedding. She held it up to Rich and said, "He might have even tied up that package with a bow on top," she said. "I wonder who Mr. O'Brien had been calling in the weeks before he died."

CHAPTER 21

CONKLIN MADE PHONE CALLS from his car as Claire supervised the transport of Arthur O'Brien's body and belongings into her van.

First he called John Sackowitz, and then he patched Brady into the call and told both of them what he knew.

He said, "It looks like O'Brien died from an accidental drug overdose. The deceased was in possession of a backpack that was a forensic lab's dream. There's a recently fired .38 with one slug left in the six-chamber cylinder and a street suppressor. Also, get this, we found a key card from the Warwick. I'm going to take a wild guess and say it opens room three twenty-one."

Sac and Brady were suitably impressed and excited.

Conklin kept going. He was on a roll.

"How'd he get the card? This, I don't know. But we have his cell phone. Maybe his call history will give up the other players in this thing. Oh, and to really seal the deal here," Conklin said, "Joan Murphy's diamonds were also in O'Brien's backpack. All of them, and they were nicely wrapped in a bandana. CSI found O'Brien's prints on all of it."

Brady said, "Good work, Inspector Conklin. Take a bow and the night off."

It was a quarter to six, so Conklin called Cindy and said, "I'll pick up a pizza." Then he sent her a phone kiss.

After that, he called Joan Murphy's phone and left a voice mail. "Joan, this is Rich Conklin. We've recovered your jewelry. There are about three pounds of diamonds here, including that pendant that I think belonged to your mother. Call me, please. We'll need you to identify it."

He clicked off and then spoke to the disconnected phone, "And by the way, Joan, I also need to talk to you about Sam Alton and Arthur O'Brien, both of whom are now deceased. You're starting to look like the center of a category 5 storm to me."

His phone buzzed.

It was Joan.

It was almost as if she'd heard him.

She said, "Hi, Richard. I'm doing all right. Keeping it together. I want to remind you that someone tried to murder me. I don't want to give this person another shot at it. You understand what I'm saying, don't you?"

"Where are you? Everyone's been worried about you. Robert called you in as a missing person."

"Never mind that. Look, Richard, the important thing is that I think I know who was behind all of this."

But then the phone went dead in his hand.

Conklin hit the Return Call button. He listened to the ringtone and got Joan's outgoing voice mail message.

"This is Joan. You know what to do."

Conklin said, "Call me back, Joan. Call me."

He got out of his car and walked over to Claire. She was shutting the back doors to the van.

"Joan just called me. She won't tell me where she is, but she said that she's staying out of harm's way. Then she hung up on me."

"Curiouser and curiouser," said Claire.

"Do you get the feeling," Rich asked Claire, "that she's making things harder for us on purpose? Why would she do that?"

CHAPTER 22

THAT NIGHT CINDY AND Rich got into bed before ten. It was an early night for them and that was a kind of blessing.

It was good to be home. Their apartment on Kirkham Street was small and cozy. They'd decorated it together so that it fit them like a hug.

Richie's arm was around Cindy, and she was wrapped around him with her cheek pressed to his chest. Streetlights sliced through the blinds, striping the walls and ceiling. Their alarm clocks were set. They each had glasses of water on their nightstands, and she had the extra blanket. Rich had the king-sized pillow behind his back.

And they had the luxury of these quiet hours to talk about their days. She loved listening to the sound of his voice.

Rich was telling her about Arthur O'Brien, the shooter who'd killed Samuel J. Alton and wounded Joan Murphy. He explained how Arthur had been the one to steal her jewelry, expose her affair, and then step off stage into the shadow of death.

"And after all this craziness about whodunnit and why," said Rich, "he keeps all the evidence in his backpack and leaves it for us to find."

"Careless," said Cindy. "It's basic hit man 101. The first thing you do is get rid of the gun."

"That's the thing, Cin. He was not a pro. Not even semi. Still, he got a key card, got an unregistered gun, shot two people, and ditched with the jewels. He got out of the hotel just like that. Shazam."

"It seems too neat," said Cindy. "How did a drug addict and occasional film extra get onto Joan and her jewels? Someone had to have put him up to it. If I had to guess, someone gave him a playbook."

"You're right. We downloaded the call log on his phone. We found a lot of stuff there, but at first look, nothing was incriminating. He called his mother regularly. He had a few friends, none of whom connected him to Alton or the Murphys. But then we found several calls to a burner phone in his call history. If he was given instructions, I bet it went through that phone. I'm thinking that if O'Brien was the shooter, he was supposed to cash in the jewels. But he flamed out before he could collect his check."

Cindy asked, "What's your next move?"

"Wait for the lab reports. Sam Alton's widow wants justice. The Murphys are out of it. Joan is alive. She has the jewelry plus a great story for all of her dinner parties, and a couple of decorative scars.

"I don't understand her," Rich continued. "I'd expect her to want me to catch the person who did this and killed Sam."

"That might be the snag," said Cindy. "Maybe she doesn't want to admit to having an affair with Sam."

"Sure. Maybe that would torpedo her marriage. But do you think that Robert doesn't know? Is he really so clueless? Or is he grilling her when the cops aren't there? Is that what's making her stick to her story? 'I was drugged and kidnapped and shot and I don't know who that hairy fat guy was who was found naked on top of me.'"

Cindy laughed and Rich joined her.

It was all so crazy.

But it was just the kind of mystery Cindy loved to solve.

CHAPTER 23

THE NEXT MORNING, CINDY and Rich said good-bye on the street and got into their cars. Rich headed to the Hall, and Cindy set her course toward Seacliff.

She didn't tell Rich where she was going. She knew what he would say. "You're poking into a police investigation. It's dangerous." Or words to that effect. Either way, it wouldn't be something she'd want to hear.

If she listened to Rich and some of her well-meaning friends, she'd be writing a fashion column. Or maybe pieces about local politics.

But she was a crime writer. Crime was not just her beat at the *Chronicle,* it was her passion. She'd written a bestselling true-crime book, sold two hundred fifty thousand copies in paperback, and had a standing offer from her publisher that he'd entertain any book ideas she might have. So, yeah.

And then she laughed out loud at the realization that she was justifying her job to herself.

She drove from her apartment through Golden Gate Park on Crossover Drive and then continued into the Richmond District toward Seacliff. She checked the house numbers on

El Camino Del Mar, a street populated with mansions and set back from the road. She slowed the car and took in the gateposts bracketing a stucco wall. This was the house. The iron gates were closed.

Cindy cruised past the house, slowing as she saw another break in the wall. This gate was also made of wrought iron, but it wasn't as wide. Only one car could fit through it at a time.

Cindy saw that there was a driveway beyond the gate. It seemed to be a service entrance, and it looked to her as though the gate had been left open.

Cindy drove farther down the road, parked her Acura on the verge, and got out. Since it was eight thirty in the morning, she had the street to herself, though she could hear the distant sound of a power tool up the road. It was either a chainsaw or blower. When one car came toward her, a Lexus with tinted windows, she busied herself on her phone until the car passed by.

Then, she crossed the road and walked directly to the service entrance gate.

Cindy pulled on the handle and the gate swung open. She slipped inside and carefully closed the gate behind her. She stopped in her tracks, looking around at the grassy lawns beyond the drive. There was a barnlike machine or tool shed to her left and beyond that a pathway of beckoning stone steps cut into a steep upward slope in the lawn.

Right now, she was "snooping," as it was called in the trade. But once she'd climbed those steps, it would no longer be fun and games. She'd have no believable excuse. It would be trespassing, plain and simple.

She stopped for a moment and put her game face on. Then she climbed up every one of those thirty steps. Technically, she wasn't breaking in. She was looking for someone to interview about a pretty interesting story that centered around a murder and the robbery of an impressive jewelry collection. If she got lucky, she'd run into Joan while she was wandering around the premises. And if she got really lucky, Joan would remember her from Claire's office.

She set out toward the pool house. It was a darling cottage with French doors that faced the pool.

Cindy reflected on what she knew about Joan. Joan had always been rich. She had owned this magnificent house before she met and married Robert Murphy, who, after all, might actually love her. And maybe she loves him, too. But anyone could make a case that something had gone horribly wrong in their marriage. That something may have caused two people to die.

Who'd done what to whom and why?

If the answer to those questions didn't make a good story, Cindy didn't know what would.

She was about to check on the pool house when a door on the side of the house opened and a man came striding toward her. He was wearing his glasses on a cord around his neck, and they bounced against his bare chest with every step he took. He wore cargo shorts, but he wasn't wearing any shoes.

And he was carrying a rifle.

A rifle that was pointed directly at Cindy's chest.

He barked, "What do you want?"

She put up her hands with her palms facing out and said, "Hold on, okay? I'm with the *Chronicle*. Joan knows me. I'm just gathering some background material on a story about the murder. Look. I have identification."

The guy looked crazy. She had opened her bag and started searching for her press pass when she heard the crack of a gunshot. Pieces of marble flew from the last stone steps in the pathway, and then with another crack, a sphere exploded at the top of a post.

Fear spiked through Cindy. She knew that words weren't going to help with this guy. He wasn't hearing her. He didn't care that she was unarmed and no threat to him. Keeping an eye on the bare-chested gunman, Cindy backed away, careful not to lose her footing on the steps below her.

But then he raised his gun and fired twice more.

Holy shit. This could not be happening. He was going to kill her, or at least give it his very best try.

Cindy knew from her experiences shooting a gun that it's a lot harder to hit a moving target than it seems on TV or in the movies. But that didn't mean that she wouldn't get shot.

As she ducked into a crouch and kept backing down the steps, her ankle turned—hard. She reached for something, anything, but she lost her balance. She made a last wild grab for another stone post, but it was too late.

Gravity was winning. She fell backward and wasn't able to

break her fall with her hands. Her head slammed against a step and her body kept rolling down, hitting stone tread after tread.

And as she completely lost consciousness before she stopped rolling on the ground, the shadow of the crazy man loomed over her.

CHAPTER 24

WHEN CLAIRE ANSWERED THE phone early that morning at the morgue, she immediately recognized the voice on the other end of the line. She asked, "Where are you, Joan?"

"About three minutes from your office, depending on the rush hour traffic. I stayed at the Intercontinental for a night. I just needed to be alone with my thoughts. Claire, I have an idea. Actually, can we talk about this in person? I'd like to invite you to breakfast at my house."

Claire genuinely liked Joan and loved to hear her laugh. She was curious about how her recovery was progressing. Not only that, but Joan was offering Claire an oceanside meal prepared by a gourmet chef plus a round-trip ride in the Bentley—and well, who could turn that down?

A few minutes later, Joan picked Claire up. As she drove them along Fell Street, she told Claire that she loved Robert.

Claire couldn't help thinking that there was going to be a *but* somewhere in Joan's story.

"I was smitten at first sight," said Joan. "He was bartending at the Redwood Room on Geary when I came in with a girl-friend from the library board. We were organizing a literary lecture series for kids. When Robert asked me to pick my poison, I told him to surprise me.

"He made me a drink, Claire, and called it a Robertini." Joan laughed and took a turn onto Stanyan Street. "I still don't know what was in it. It was layered in many colors and smelled like a garden in the rain. That's what it tasted like, too, but it had a secret punch at the end."

Claire was enjoying the romantic meet-cute story, but she was still waiting for the *but*.

"We started dating. He was very demonstrative and funny. He could do impressions, you know. His George W. Bush was hilarious, and his impression of me—my God." Joan laughed long and hard. "Maybe he'll do it for you. You won't believe how spot-on it is.

"But most important, I could tell Robbie anything and everything. I felt completely comfortable around him. I told him about my first marriage to Jared, and how the man I loved had turned out to be gay. That's when Robert said, 'I got news for you, Joanie. I play for that team, too.'"

Claire exhaled. So that was the *but*. She said, "And the two of you decided to get married anyway?"

"It worked for Judy Garland." Joan laughed. "Look, I love Robbie. He is handsome, don't you think?"

"Very."

"He's very talented, too. He can sing and dance. And he can act like that guy on NCIS. Mark Harmon."

"Impressive," said Claire.

Joan nodded and pulled the large silver Bentley up to the gates to her home. She held the remote out the window with her good arm, pressed the button on it, and the gates swung in. She drove up to the beautiful house and parked next to a Mercedes sedan.

"I got that for Robbie for our anniversary. The two of us have a good marriage." Joan turned off the car and faced Claire. "That's why I know that Robert didn't try to kill me, Claire. He doesn't want to be a widower. He's pretty obsessed with his image, and that title would make him seem old. Besides, he and I have nothing but good times. We don't fight. We have love and companionship. Honestly, that's all we need."

"And Samuel Alton?"

"Who? Say, is that coffee and something yummy I smell?"

Claire opened her car door and Joan reached over to the glove box with her bandaged arm. She took out a pistol.

Claire said, "Whoa. What's that for?"

Joan shrugged and said, "Someone tried to murder me, remember?" Then she grinned and started waving the gun like a rodeo clown as she took Claire around the side of the house and out to the patio.

Once they sat down at the table, Marjorie came out and said, "Welcome, Dr. Washburn. Would you like a mimosa to start?"

Claire said, "I'll have orange juice without the champagne, please. I have to go back to work after breakfast."

Joan was standing at the edge of the patio, sighting various objects on the property over the top of her gun, from the statuary to specimen trees to the birds. Each time she aimed her gun at something, she said, *"Pytoo, pytoo, pytoo."*

Claire said, "Joan? Is that thing loaded?"

Joan called back, "Of course it is. I've also got a license, if you're wondering, and I've gone out to the range to practice. You can never be too careful when you were almost murdered."

"Come sit down and give me that thing. I'll give it back after I leave, okay? It's just for my own safety, get me?"

"You're silly," Joan said, laughing, but she sat down and put the gun on the table. The muzzle was pointing in Claire's direction. Claire gently spun the gun so it was pointing toward the horizon.

She let out a small breath, but her heart kept beating wildly in her chest.

Marjorie brought out the breakfast. It was a mushroom and fines herbes frittata that smelled delicious and was paired with a side of oven-fresh warm bread. Claire's stomach rumbled, so she unfurled her napkin and placed it in her lap. She was just lifting her fork when she heard what sounded like a gunshot.

"What's that?" Claire asked.

Two more shots were fired.

"It's coming from the pool house. Damn it to hell!"

Then Joan grabbed the pistol and started to run.

CHAPTER 25

CLAIRE STOOD UP FAST. She knocked over a chair, hit the table with her hip, and scattered the contents of the dishes and the juice in the wineglasses. She started moving, doing her best to catch up to Joan. The woman was her age but slimmer, and even with her clipped wing, Joan was faster and more athletic than Claire.

She called out to her, "Joan, wait up!"

But Joan was not listening.

Claire huffed behind her, crossing the lawn. She saw a cottage to her left, a swimming pool, and a set of meandering stone stairs. There was a man standing at the top of it with a rifle. He had the gun sight up to his eye as he pointed it down the steps.

Joan yelled, "Peter! Peter, stop what you're doing! Right now!"

The man whom Joan called Peter was fit and bare-chested. A pair of glasses was hanging from the cord around his neck, and he was wearing a pair of khaki shorts. When he heard Joan calling him, he turned toward her, but only slightly. He hardly lowered the gun at all, maybe just a few degrees. And he certainly didn't drop it.

Joan was still holding her pistol. And she raised it and pointed it at Peter.

It was a standoff. But how long would it last?

Claire pictured the horrible scene that was about to happen in front of her.

But then she had an idea, albeit untested. She called out, using the most authoritative voice she had.

"Everyone freeze."

She heard a groaning noise coming from the edge of the steps, where Peter had pointed his rifle and had likely fired the three shots. It sounded almost human. Had he shot someone? Was that person lying down there?

"Peter," Joan called out from forty feet away. "You'd better put that gun down. I figured out what you did. I know that it was you all along. And if you drop that gun, we can talk about it."

Again, Peter lifted the gun sight to his eye. This time, he was aiming his rifle directly at Joan. But before he could squeeze off a shot, Joan fired.

Not once, but three times.

And the sound of the gun was not *pytoo, pytoo, pytoo*.

It was *BAM, BAM, BAM*.

The sound was deafening, and the aftershocks echoed off the exterior walls of the tiny cottage. Peter yelped, grabbed his gut, and went down to the ground. His body curled into a ball.

At that moment, a man came galloping across the lawn from the direction of the main house.

And he was screaming, "Peter, Peter! Oh, my God, Joan! You shot Peter!"

CHAPTER 26

CLAIRE HAD LEFT HER handbag at the breakfast table, which meant that she didn't have a phone on her.

Holy shit, she didn't have a phone.

She ran past Joan over to the man called Peter, who was on his back on the grass. The other man, whom Claire took to be Robert Murphy, was cradling Peter's head and pleading with him, asking him not to die.

A quick visual exam told Claire that Peter had taken a shot under his rib cage. The man was probably bleeding internally. He'd taken another bullet to his left thigh, which was spouting blood like a small fire hose.

Peter was conscious, and he seemed to be in excruciating pain. In between moans, he was gasping to Robert, "It had to be done. I had to do it."

What was he talking about?

Claire directed Robert to take off his belt so he could make a tourniquet above the bullet hole in Peter's thigh.

"Robert, cinch it and hold it tight. Good. I'm going to make sure an ambulance is on the way. Do not let him move. Do you hear me?"

Robert nodded. Tears were running down his cheeks. "He has PTSD. From a stint he did in Afghanistan."

"I don't understand."

"He freaks out sometimes. Jesus Christ. Peter."

Claire told Robert to try to keep Peter calm. Then she stood up to look for Joan.

And she saw her. Joan was walking back toward the house at a leisurely pace. She was still holding the gun at her side. She'd simply turned her back on the bloody, awful scene that had blown up in her own backyard. All because of the gunshots she'd fired.

But in Claire's opinion, Joan had shot Peter in self-defense. Those shots had saved her life and probably Claire's, too. She must be in shock. That was understandable. But now that a man's life was on the line, Joan had to snap out of it.

Claire yelled, "Joan! Call an ambulance!"

"Okay," said Joan. But she didn't quicken her pace. She just continued to stroll up the soft, grassy lawns toward the house.

"Joan, they don't call this a matter of life and death for no reason! If you don't hurry up, Peter could actually die!"

Joan turned and seemed to give Claire's words some thought. Then she shrugged her shoulders and said, "There's a landline in the pool house."

"Make the call," Claire said. "Damn it, Joan! Run!"

Claire's mind was reeling. She obviously couldn't count on Joan to do what needed to be done, and she didn't know if she could count on Robert to help her, either. Claire was surrounded by eccentrics when she needed an ambulance filled with professionals and a platoon of cops.

She went back to Robert and Peter. Robert had completely lost his cool. As far as Claire could tell, he wasn't acting. Clearly, he cared a lot about the man in his arms—and that man was currently pale, sweaty, and losing consciousness. She told Robert, "Joan is calling an ambulance." Honestly, she couldn't be confident that Joan had listened to her, but she hoped the news would calm Robert down.

Claire walked toward the street and looked out over a grassy hillock and the stone staircase that led toward the drive, the gates, and the street.

She was completely unprepared to see a woman's body sprawled out on the stairs, her head facing toward the bottom.

Oh, my God. Peter had killed someone.

Of course. She and Joan had heard shots at breakfast, and they had been fatal. Claire ran toward the body, and once she got closer, her heart almost stopped.

It couldn't be true, but it was.

The woman on the steps had a blond mop of curls and her entire outfit was baby blue. It was Cindy.

And she was lying motionless on the ground.

Please. Don't let her be dead.

CHAPTER 27

CLAIRE KNELT DOWN BESIDE her friend. There was blood at Cindy's temple. A head wound. But Claire could see the gentle rise and fall of Cindy's chest. Her friend was still breathing.

Claire felt her pulse. It was strong. *Thank you, Lord.*

"Cindy, can you hear me? It's me, Claire."

She gently turned Cindy's head and looked for the source of the blood. She was covered in it. It was running from her temple, down her neck, and into her sweater. Had Cindy been shot in the head?

But then Claire found it. Four inches behind the temple, at the back of her head, was a bloody gash. Not a hole. Claire parted Cindy's hair and saw that the laceration looked like it had been caused by Cindy's fall. She must have hit her head on the edge of a stone tread.

Claire put her hands on Cindy's shoulders.

"Cindy. It's Claire. Can you hear me?"

Cindy groaned and Claire said, "Thank you, God."

"Claire? What happened?"

"Put your arms around my neck."

Cindy reached up, and Claire helped her friend into a more

comfortable position. She sat her on a step, and leaned her back against the edge of the wall.

"How do you feel?"

"My head hurts. And I think I twisted my ankle."

"Aw, Cindy. I'm here. I'm here." Claire patted her friend's back.

Claire saw Cindy's handbag below the steps, lying on the grass. She ran down to get it, opened the hobo bag, and poured out the contents. She pawed through the litter of purse junk until she found it.

Cindy's cell phone. She checked the battery. The phone was charged.

Next, she dialed the radio room at the Hall and let out a breath of relief when she got the voice of dispatcher May Hess. May knew every cop in the Southern Station. And she knew everyone in the ME's office, as well. Claire was in good hands.

"May, this is Claire Washburn and I'm reporting an emergency. I need an ambulance pronto to 420 El Camino Del Mar. We've got a man bleeding out from multiple gunshots. And we have another victim here with a head injury. When I say pronto, I mean it. Get everyone moving at the speed of light."

When she clicked off with dispatch, Claire called Richie, cursing silently when the call went to voice mail. "Rich, I'm at Joan Murphy's house. Cindy is here. She's taken a fall and is a little shaken up, but she's going to be okay.

"Also, Rich, the pool boy who goes by the name of Peter was about to fire on Joan but she shot him first. Twice.

"An ambulance is on the way. Listen, Rich, I think Robert Murphy might be involved with Peter. And it seems that Peter may have knowledge of the Warwick Hotel shooting. He might tell you what he knows. But on the other hand, there's a good chance he might die. And soon."

CHAPTER 28

CLAIRE LISTENED FOR THE sound of sirens.

Only four minutes had passed since she'd called dispatch, but each minute was critical. She needed to get Peter into emergency care alive.

Robert was still cradling Peter's head in his lap. He was also holding his hand, stroking his hair, and telling him that he would be fine. But as the soothing words left his mouth, Robert shot a questioning look at Claire, looking for verification that Peter would survive.

She nodded but couldn't fully commit to her answer. The man's shorts were soaked with blood. Despite the tourniquet, Peter was hemorrhaging. He could very easily bleed out if help didn't arrive soon.

"The ambulance will be here in a minute. I'll be right over there with the other victim."

She walked back to the staircase where Cindy was reclining against the stone wall, breathing normally. Her bleeding had stopped. Thank goodness.

Claire wrapped her in a big, comforting hug, saying, "Richie is on his way."

Cindy smiled and said, "Oh, good." But then her face crumpled and she started to cry. Claire hugged her friend more tightly and then pulled back to look into her face. Cindy's sobs had turned into laughter that was now verging on hysteria.

"What's going on, Cindy?"

"I'm just overwhelmed," Cindy admitted. "What if you hadn't found me here? Who knows what would have happened to me."

"I know, Cindy, I know," Claire murmured, patting Cindy's back some more.

But then Cindy shook her head and put on her tough face. She wiped her tears and said, "How is it that I missed all the action? Can you tell me that?"

"You're alive, dummy," Claire said. "Could you just be happy that you're alive?"

Their playful exchange was interrupted by a woman's voice that said, "Claire?"

It was Joan. She was walking down the steps, looking cute and unconcerned. It was almost as if she had a new role in a movie and had just walked out onto the set, thinking she could wing her lines.

"Wait, is that Cindy next to you?" she asked.

Cindy said, "Claire, help me up."

"Stay where you are, sweetie. It's better if you sit still until the paramedics arrive. Unlike me, they have medical equipment and will be able to check you out properly."

Joan said, "Cindy, what happened to you?"

"A man up there tried to shoot me. I ducked, but then I also tripped and fell down these steps. It was silly, really. Claire says I'm going to live."

Joan groaned and said, "Oh, that freaking Peter. He's a maniac." She sat down next to Cindy and took her hand.

She turned her head up to look at Claire and said, "I wanted to tell you that those gunshots jogged a memory. Sam Alton. I remember him now."

With those words, she instantly had Claire and Cindy's avid attention.

"I guess you could say he was my boyfriend. We didn't use our real names with each other. I called him Butchie. He called me Princess. We kept each other company from time to time, but it wasn't love between us. Our relationship came out of pure and simple need, on both of our parts." She cleared her throat and sighed, saying, "Still. He was very kind and he didn't deserve to die. I'm so very sorry that he's dead. I never saw who shot him, but I know that Peter has to have been involved. I wish I had seen Butchie's killer. I wish I knew how it happened."

Sirens wailed, amped up, and stopped as an ambulance drove up to the service gate at the bottom of the steps.

Joan and Claire both stood up.

There were the sounds of panel doors slamming and voices shouting. Claire ran down to the driveway and helped the team by opening the gate for them so they could carry a stretcher through.

"Hurry," she yelled. "We need you up here."

CHAPTER 29

INSPECTOR RICHARD CONKLIN WAS conducting a bedside interview at St. Francis Memorial Hospital for the second time this week. But this time, it was more than that. This interview was an official interrogation.

Peter Carter had gone through surgery, had cleared the recovery room, and was now settled in his private room. Hours earlier, his surgeon had pronounced him in stable condition.

Conklin had arrested Carter for his attempt on Joan Murphy's life. If the force was with Conklin, the dangerous fool in the hospital bed was going to admit to being part of a conspiracy to murder Joan Murphy—twice—as well as the plan to murder Joan's friend and proven lover, Sam Alton.

Right now, Peter Carter was in a talkative mood. His hand was cuffed to his bed rail. His eyes were closed, and the sheets were pulled up under his arms. His leg was in a cast and in traction. Prior to this interview, Conklin learned that this man was a person who couldn't shoot straight without his glasses. To Conklin, Peter Carter looked like an ordinary and even pleasant man.

"Feeling okay to talk?" Conklin asked.

"Only if you promise not to judge me," the man said.

"I'm not like that," said Conklin. "I just want to clear up a few things. Before we start, though, I want to make sure you understand your rights."

"Okay. I told you already. I understand them."

"Fine. And I'm going to keep recording our conversation on my phone." He showed the phone to Carter, then set it down on the tray table.

Carter said he understood his rights and Conklin believed him. He also believed that Carter was desperate to be understood and forgiven so that he could return to something like life as he had known it.

But that wasn't going to happen.

Conklin said, "I want to start in the middle, Peter. Look, you should know that Arthur O'Brien is dead. He overdosed in his apartment."

"No way. Are you shitting me?"

"Sorry. I know he was a friend. We have his cell phone and have the phone records. He called you many times while you two planned the hit on Joan at the Warwick. What I don't know is how it all went wrong."

Carter sighed. "Damn it. I told him to always call my prepaid phone. I guess I didn't realize that he'd called me on my cell."

At Carter's words, Conklin silently congratulated himself. He hadn't been positively sure of the connection between these two men until this minute. *Thanks for confirming the conspiracy, bud.*

He said, "People can get rattled. Sometimes they make mistakes when they're doing something they're not used to doing, right?"

Carter agreed. He said, "Artie was an old school friend. I knew I could trust him. He needed the money. He isn't, you know, a professional."

"Sure. We get that. So he was supposed to kill Joan and keep the jewelry, right? But why kill her? Help me to understand."

"I didn't have a choice. Robert doesn't love Joan. He's told me so many times that he loves me, but I know he'll never leave her. I thought if she just happened to die while she was on a date with someone else, he'd be a free man. He'd own the house and we…"

Carter trailed off. Conklin didn't want him to fall asleep. Not now. "Peter. Peter, I'm still here."

CHAPTER 30

CONKLIN REACHED OVER AND shook Peter Carter's arm, keeping him awake before he slipped into a post-operative slumber.

His eyes opened. "Oh. It's you. What was I saying?"

"You were saying that you got Arthur to kill Joan?"

"Well, yeah. Better him than me. I wanted to have a clean conscience. A clean enough conscience, anyway. I mean, if I didn't actually shoot her…"

He winced from pain, looked at the water glass on the tray table. Conklin handed it to Carter and watched while he drank, sputtered, then handed the glass back to Conklin.

Conklin asked, "And what about Samuel Alton? Was killing him in the original plan?"

Carter nodded.

"That's yes?"

"Yes. It wasn't anything personal. He was just collateral damage. It had to be done."

"I see. I understand all that. You had to kill the witness, right?"

Carter nodded, winced, and then closed his eyes.

Conklin said, "Peter. Is that a yes?"

"Yes. For God's sake, are you thick? I think it's time for me to take a nap. Where's Robert?"

Conklin didn't want to answer that one. Because Robert Murphy was a material witness, Conklin's team had him in lockup. Sac and Linden were questioning him, but charges had not yet been brought to the table.

Meanwhile, Conklin pressed on with his interrogation. "Peter, Robert will be in to see you later. I'm sure of it. But for now, we have to finish here. Understand?"

"Go ahead, then," Carter said. "I'm in a lot of pain, man. Let's get this over with."

"Good," said Conklin. "Two more minutes. That's all."

Peter asked, "What was the question?"

"The key card," Conklin said. "We have the key card to Joan's hotel room. It was in Artie's possession. How on earth did Artie get that?"

"Right," said Carter. "That was easy. I went to the Warwick. I paid off the guy at the front desk and told him I just wanted to take pictures. I showed him my camera, and I said, 'One picture is worth a thousand buckaroos.' I didn't have to ask twice. The guy made me a key and even put on this big show of welcoming me to the Warwick. Ha!

"Then I handed that key card off to my buddy Artie. An hour later, he calls and tells me that he'd done the job and that it had gone off perfectly. He was in and out in three minutes. It was such a relief. I figured that after that call, it was all over, except for the funeral, of course. But then, Joan comes home with gunshot wounds. She walks. She talks. She seems to be just about as good as new."

"Huh," said Rich. "That must have been a shock for you."

Carter went on. "She completely wrecked it, man. Everything I'd worked so hard to coordinate. Hey, what's your name again?"

"Conklin. Inspector Richard Conklin."

Carter waved his hand as if Conklin's name was unimportant, after all. He was into his story, though. He wanted to complain.

"The whole situation between me and Robert worked for two years—but then all of a sudden, Joan wouldn't allow it anymore. Like, who gave her the right to say whether the relationship between me and my boyfriend is okay or not? Look, if you really want to know who was behind all this, it was Joan herself. She was the one who started it. She should have left us alone. Okay? Are we done now?"

Conklin knew it was now or maybe never again. The answer to this question was critical.

"So, Peter, you're saying that Robert had knowledge of this plan to kill Joan?"

"No, no. I didn't tell him about that. You gotta be kidding me. She caused it, but it was my plan all along. I figured with Joan out of the way, Robert and I could be happy. I never wanted him to know what I'd done to Joan. Correction, tried to do to her. Honest to God, that's the whole truth. Robert had absolutely no part in it."

"Okay," said Conklin. "I believe you."

"What happens next?" Peter asked.

"Get some sleep. And then you'll want to get a good lawyer."

"Call Robert, will you?"

"Sure."

Peter Carter had relaxed back into a dopey, angelic post-operative doze when Conklin said, "Take care."

Then he left the room with the taped confession in his pocket and said good night to the two officers on guard outside the door.

CHAPTER 31

CINDY WAS IN AN excellent mood.

Her editor, Henry Tyler, had been so happy with "A Miraculous Life." It was her first-person account of Joan Murphy's ordeal. In fact, Henry had liked the article so much that he'd ceremoniously presented her with a little statuette from the fifties that he kept in his office called the Smith Corona. The bone-china figurine depicted a high-stepping young woman in a business suit who wore a typewriter as a hat.

"This, Cindy, this is how I think of you."

She'd laughed and thrown her arms around Henry. She told him that getting the Smith Corona was better than getting an Oscar. And it was. She surrounded the statuette with a forest of candlesticks on the sideboard.

In a couple of hours, she and Rich were having a special dinner in their small, ground-floor apartment to welcome home Lindsay and Joe, who had just returned from their vacation yesterday.

They decided to make the theme of the party "Thanksgiving dinner," because the meal was so good that they didn't want to wait until November to enjoy it. In preparation for their version of turkey day, Cindy had asked Claire to bring cranberry sauce, a vegetable side, and stuffing. Rich had stepped up to make his Thanksgiving specialty of the house since childhood: a yam casserole with marshmallows on top.

Brady had said, "Do not worry about wine. I will take care of the alcohol course, trust me." And Yuki had added, "I can bring garlands with popcorn and cranberries. Believe it or not, I think I saw some of them out at the market this week. Even though it isn't November, we have to make it look festive."

The meal was going to be excellent.

Cindy had roasted the turkey, basting it properly, leaving enough time for the meat to cool before her guests arrived. Richie made his yams and set up the table in the dining room, adding in the extensions they'd never used before.

They had finally gotten the table ready for everyone when the doorbell rang.

Claire and Edmund arrived first, carrying covered dishes. After Rich hung up their coats, they went into the kitchen to help Cindy and warm up their hot side. Claire had an exquisite talent with a carving knife, and as she dissected the turkey, she explained each and every one of her cuts. It sent Cindy into fits of laughter.

Yuki and Brady showed up with wine and the promised garlands, and Brady hoisted Yuki up so that she could tack the garlands to the ceiling and string them across the tops of bookcases. He spun her around a couple of times, and she scissored her legs as if she were a ballerina. Everyone enjoyed the spectacle.

When the doorbell rang again, Cindy opened the door.

Lindsay, Joe, and Julie came through the doorway. Lindsay held up three boxes and said, "I hope triple-chocolate cake is okay. We have a couple of pies for everyone, too. It's all store-bought though. I'm still in vacation mode."

"Cake and pie," Cindy gushed, and she took the treats from her friend. "That's fantastic."

A shout went up when the Molinari family entered the living room. "Yay! The gang's all here."

Everyone hugged Lindsay, Joe, and Julie. Even though it had only been a week, it somehow felt like more time had passed.

Brady opened wine bottles and poured glasses for the adults, while Cindy got a cup of milk for Julie. She asked the toddler if she was she glad to be home and smiled when Julie nodded emphatically.

Rich assembled eight assorted chairs in the living room and passed around the nuts and a cheese platter. While everyone munched on their snacks, they caught up and told stories and jokes.

After appetizers, everyone moved into the dining room. Once they were all settled around the table, with Julie sitting next to Joe on a kitchen stool, Edmund thanked God for their good health and wonderful friendships.

After the amens, Brady suggested they all go around the table and say what they're thankful for, as if it were actually Thanksgiving. Everyone thought it was a great idea. He went first and said, "I'm thankful to be married to Yuki and for knowin' all a y'all. I swear to God."

Joe popped into the kitchen and came back with the turkey. He set it on the table. "It's trite but true," he said, "that I am glad for this big turkey."

Edmund said, "Cindy, I am thankful you got Claire to make her chestnut stuffing because we haven't had it in about five years."

Claire laughed and said, "That's not true." Then she followed up her protestations by saying, "I'm thankful for you, too, Edmund, and for 'all a y'all,'" which got a long round of laughter from the group.

When the laughing finally subsided, Claire added, "And I'm really happy that my folks sent me to medical school. Look where it got me. *Bon appétit,* everyone."

It was a short reach across the table for all to clink glasses, which they did.

Lindsay said, "I'm thankful to Cindy for taking care of Martha while I was away and for putting together this wonderful Thanksgiving dinner. It was such a good idea to celebrate with a turkey. But I'm also wondering what I've missed. Did anything happen? At all?"

Conklin said, "Nah. Nothing."

"Not much," said Cindy. But then she leaned in closer

to Lindsay and added, "We were just on the juiciest case ever."

"Are you kidding me?" said Lindsay.

"Well," said Cindy, "It was in the top ten, anyway."

And Claire said, "It was definitely a murder case for the ages."

EPILOGUE

CLAIRE WAS THE FIRST to open Joan's handwritten invitation for holiday drinks with her new friends, saying it was a "surprise" venue that was for "girls only."

Claire called Cindy, Lindsay, and Yuki, and they were all in.

A driver picked them each up from their offices and drove them out to the Pier 39 Marina at Fisherman's Wharf. The car was a Bentley, and Cindy immediately located the champagne in an ice bucket in the backseat of the car, which made the ride merry and bright.

After a short while, the driver delivered the Women's Murder Club to a slip of land, where Joan and Marjorie were waiting for them. Joan was bundled up in charcoal cashmere and had her mother's large diamond pendant around her neck.

The night was cool, but it wasn't cold, and the sky was clear, providing a beautiful backdrop for the marina. There were at least three hundred double-fingered boat slips docked along the pier, and the women took in incredible views of Alcatraz and the Golden Gate Bridge.

Joan embraced each of her guests, including Lindsay, whom

she'd never met. "I've heard so much about you," she said, giving her shoulders an extra squeeze.

"I've heard a bit about you, too," Lindsay said.

They laughed and hugged again.

A gorgeous motor yacht pulled up in front of them. It was a seventy-two-foot cabin cruiser with a long, open bridge and old-fashioned brass lights hung along the teakwood trim. The captain's name was Gina Marie, and she looked impeccable in her white uniform and red lipstick. She gave each of them a wide smile as she welcomed them aboard.

Lindsay and Cindy cast off the lines, and Gina Marie started up the engine. Then the guests went down to the lounge, where Marjorie served champagne and hors d'oeuvres. She sat next to Joan when everyone was served and joined the festivities. But the question still lingered: what was the occasion?

Once the yacht was skimming the bay at a comfortable ten knots, Joan stood up with her glass in her hand.

Claire thought Joan looked lighter and happier than she'd seen her three months before. She'd healed well. Her hair was longer and blonder. The scarf around her neck flew like a pendant over her shoulder. Her many diamonds sparkled like stars.

"I have an important announcement to make," she said.

Everyone looked up at Joan.

"I've asked Robert to move out of the house. And I've filed for divorce, which I think I'll be able to get without any problems."

Claire said, "Wow."

Cindy echoed the "wow," adding, "Way to go, Joan."

Joan laughed and then lifted her glass. "So I want to make a toast to all of you. Here's to friendship."

It was difficult to maintain their balance on the moving yacht, but everyone stood up to hug each other.

For the rest of the ride, no one answered a phone. Dinner was delicious and memorable. Joan entertained the women with stories from her fabulous life. She'd rubbed shoulders with many celebrities over the years, and even clued the ladies in to a secret romance that she had with a very elusive actor.

There was clapping and laughter and champagne toasts to round out a great celebratory girls' night.

The first, it felt, of many to come.

ABOUT THE AUTHORS

JAMES PATTERSON has written more bestsellers and created more enduring fictional characters than any other novelist writing today. He lives in Florida with his family.

MAXINE PAETRO has collaborated with James Patterson on the bestselling Women's Murder Club and Private series. She lives with her husband in New York State.

THE DOLLS ARE PERFECT LOVERS, PERFECT COMPANIONS, *PERFECT KILLERS.*

Investigative reporter Lana Wallace has covered many crimes of passion in ten years. But nothing will prepare her for the dark secrets of… *The Dolls.*

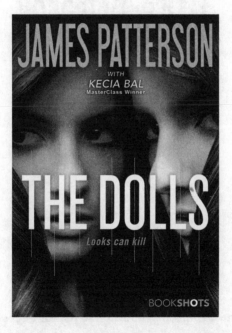

Read the spine-tingling new thriller, *The Dolls,* available only from

BOOK**SHOTS**

DR. CROSS, THE SUSPECT IS YOUR PATIENT.

An anonymous caller has promised to set off deadly bombs in Washington, DC. A cruel hoax or the real deal? By the time Alex Cross and his wife, Bree Stone, uncover the chilling truth, it may already be too late....

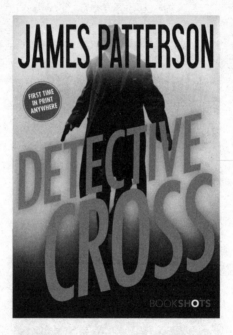

Read the thrilling new addition to the Alex Cross series,
Detective Cross, **available only from**

BOOKSHOTS

MONEY. BETRAYAL. MURDER.
THAT'S A *PRIVATE* CONVERSATION.

Hired to protect a visiting American woman, Private
Johannesburg's Joey Montague is hoping for a routine job
looking after a nervous tourist. After the apparent suicide of his
business partner, he can't handle much more. But this case is not
what it seems—and neither is his partner's death.

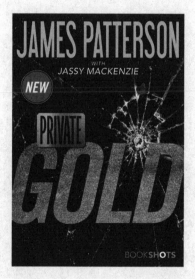

Read the thrilling new addition to the Private series,
Private: Gold, **available only from**

BOOK**SHOTS**

BONJOUR, DETECTIVE LUC MONCRIEF.
NOW WATCH YOUR BACK.

Very handsome and charming French detective Luc Moncrief joined the NYPD for a fresh start—but someone wants to make his first big case his last.

Welcome to New York.

**Read all of the heart-pounding thrillers in the
Luc Moncrief series:**
French Kiss
The Christmas Mystery
French Twist
Available only from

BOOK**SHOTS**

HE'S WORTH MILLIONS...
BUT HE'S WORTHLESS WITHOUT HER.

Siobhan Dempsey came to New York with a purpose: she wants
to become a successful artist. But then she meets tech billionaire
Derick Miller, who takes her breath away. And though Siobhan's
body comes alive at his touch, their relationship has been a
roller-coaster ride.

Are they meant to be together?

Read the steamy Diamond Trilogy books:

Dazzling: The Diamond Trilogy, Book I
Radiant: The Diamond Trilogy, Book II
Exquisite: The Diamond Trilogy, Book III

Available only from